DON'T GO TO SLEEP!

Look for more Goosebumps books
by R.L. Stine:
(see back of book for a complete listing)

Goosebumps®

DON'T GO TO SLEEP!

R.L. STINE

AN
APPLE
PAPERBACK

SCHOLASTIC INC.
New York Toronto London Auckland Sydney

A PARACHUTE PRESS BOOK

If you purchased this book without a cover, you should be aware that this book is stolen property. It was reported as "unsold and destroyed" to the publisher, and neither the author nor the publisher has received any payment for this "stripped book."

No part of this publication may be reproduced in whole or in part, or stored in a retrieval system, or transmitted in any form or by any means, electronic, mechanical, photocopying, recording, or otherwise, without written permission of the publisher. For information regarding permission, write to Scholastic Inc., 555 Broadway, New York, NY 10012.

ISBN 0-590-56891-4

Copyright © 1997 by Parachute Press, Inc.
All rights reserved. Published by Scholastic Inc.
APPLE PAPERBACKS and the APPLE PAPERBACKS logo are registered trademarks of Scholastic Inc.
GOOSEBUMPS is a registered trademark
of Parachute Press, Inc.

12 11 10 9 8 7 6 5 4 3 2 1   7 8 9/9 0 1 2/0

Printed in the U.S.A.   40

First Scholastic printing, April 1997

DON'T GO TO SLEEP! .

Klonk! "Ow! The Klingon got me!"

I rubbed my head and kicked my life-sized photo of a Klingon — one of those warlike aliens on *Star Trek* — out of the way. I'd been reaching for one of my favorite books, *Ant Attack on Pluto,* when the big hunk of cardboard fell off the top shelf and klonked me on the head.

I kicked the Klingon again. "Take that, you evil piece of cardboard!"

I was fed up. My stuff kept attacking me.

My room was packed with junk. Things were always leaping off the walls and whacking me on the head. This wasn't the first time.

"Uhn!" I gave the Klingon another kick for good measure.

"Matthew Amsterdam, twelve-year-old geek." My older brother, Greg, stood in my bedroom doorway, murmuring into a tape recorder.

"Get out of my room!" I grumbled.

Greg totally ignored me. He always does.

"Matt is skinny, small for his age, with a round, piglike baby face," he said. He was still talking into the tape recorder.

"Matt's hair is so blond that, from a distance, he almost looks bald." Greg spoke in a deep, fake voice. He was trying to sound like the guy who describes animals on those nature shows.

"At least I don't have a Brillo pad sitting on my head," I cracked.

Greg and my sister, Pam, both have wiry brown hair. Mine is white-blond and really thin. Mom says my dad had the same hair as me. But I don't remember him. He died when I was a baby.

Greg smirked at me and went on in that *Wild Kingdom* voice. "Matt's natural habitat is a small bedroom filled with science-fiction books, models of alien spacecraft, comic books, dirty socks, rotten pizza crusts, and other geekazoid stuff. How can Matt can stand it? Scientists are puzzled by this. Remember, geeks have always been a mystery to normal humans."

"I'd rather be a geek than a nerd like you," I said.

"You're not smart enough to be a nerd," he shot back in his regular voice.

My sister, Pam, appeared beside him in the doorway. "What's happening here in Geek World?" she asked. "Did the mother ship finally come for you, Matt?"

I threw *Ant Attack on Pluto* at her.

Pam is in tenth grade. Greg is in eleventh. They gang up on me all the time.

Greg spoke into his tape recorder again. "When threatened, the geek *will* attack. However, he is about as dangerous as a bowl of mashed potatoes."

"Get out!" I yelled. I tried to close the door, but they blocked it.

"I can't leave," Greg protested. "I have a school project. I have to watch everybody in the family and write a paper about how they act. It's for social studies."

"Go watch Pam pick her nose," I snapped.

Pam knocked Greg aside and pushed her way into the room. She grabbed me by the neck of my *Star Trek* T-shirt.

"Take that back!" she ordered.

"Let go!" I cried. "You're stretching out my shirt!"

"Matthew is very touchy about his geek clothes," Greg mumbled into the recorder.

"I said, take that back!" Pam shook me. "Or I'll sic Biggie on you!"

Biggie is our dog. He's not big — he's a dachshund. But he hates me for some reason.

With everybody else — even total strangers — he wags his tail, licks their hands, the whole bit. With me, he growls and snaps.

3

Once Biggie sneaked into my room and bit me in my sleep. I'm a heavy sleeper — it takes a lot to wake me up. But believe me, when a dog bites you, you wake up.

"Here, Biggie!" Pam called.

"Okay!" I cried. "I take it back."

"Good answer," Pam said. "You win the noogie prize!" She started knocking me on the head.

"Ow! Ow!" I gasped.

"The geek's sister gives him noogies to the head," Greg commented. "Geek says, 'Ow.'"

Finally Pam let me go. I stumbled and collapsed on my bed. The bed knocked against the wall. A pile of books rained down on me from the shelf over my head.

"Give me that tape recorder for a second," Pam said to Greg. She snatched it from him and yelled into the microphone. "The geek is down! Thanks to me, Pamela Amsterdam, the world is safe for cool people again! Woo! Woo! Woo!"

I hate my life.

Pam and Greg use me as their human punching bag. Maybe if Mom were around more, she'd be able to stop them.

But she is hardly ever around. She works two jobs. Her day job is teaching people how to use computers. And her night job is typing at a law firm.

Pam and Greg are supposed to be taking care of me. They take care of me, all right.

4

They make sure I'm miserable twenty-four hours a day.

"This room stinks," Pam groaned. "Let's get out of here, Greg."

They slammed the door behind them. My model space shuttle fell off the dresser and crashed to the floor.

At least they left me alone. I didn't care what mean things they said, as long as they went away.

I settled on my bed to read *Ant Attack on Pluto*. I'd much rather be on the planet Pluto than in my own house — even with giant ants shooting spit rays at me.

My bed felt lumpy. I shoved a bunch of books and clothes to the floor.

I had the smallest bedroom in the house — of course. I always got the worst of everything. Even the guest room was bigger than my room.

I didn't understand it. I needed a big room more than anybody! I had so many books, posters, models, and other junk that there was barely room for me to sleep.

I opened my book and started reading. I came to a really scary part. Justin Case, a human space traveler, was captured by the evil ant emperor. The ant emperor closed in on him, closer, closer . . .

I shut my eyes for a second — just a second — but I guess I fell asleep. Suddenly I felt the ant emperor's hot, stinking breath on my face!

Ugh! It smelled exactly like dog food.

Then I heard growling.

I opened my eyes.

It was worse than I thought. Worse than an ant emperor.

It was Biggie — ready to spring!

2

"Biggie!" I screamed. "Get off me!"

Snap! He attacked me with his gaping dachshund jaws.

I dodged him — he missed me. I shoved him off the bed.

He snarled at me and tried to jump back up. He was too short. He couldn't reach the bed without taking a running leap.

I stood on the bed. Biggie snapped at my feet. "Help!" I yelled.

That's when I saw Pam and Greg in the doorway, laughing their heads off.

Biggie backed up to take his running jump. "Help me, you guys!" I begged.

"Yeah, right," Pam said. Greg doubled over laughing.

"Come on," I whined. "I can't get down! He'll bite me!"

Greg gasped for breath. "Why do you think we

put him on your bed in the first place? Ha-ha-ha-ha!"

"You shouldn't sleep so much, Matt," Greg said. "We thought we had to wake you up."

"Besides, we were bored," Pam added. "We wanted to have some fun."

Biggie galloped across the room and leaped onto the bed. As he jumped up, I jumped down. I scurried across the floor — slipping on comic books as I ran.

Biggie raced after me. I ducked into the hallway and slammed the door just before he got out.

Biggie barked like crazy.

"Let him out, Matt!" Pam scolded me. "How can you be so mean to poor, sweet Biggie?"

"Leave me alone!" I shouted. I ran downstairs to the living room. I plopped myself on the couch and flicked on the TV. I didn't bother to surf — I always watch the same channel. The Sci-Fi channel.

I heard Biggie bounding down the steps. I tensed, waiting for him to attack. But he waddled into the kitchen.

Probably going to eat some disgusting doggie treats, I thought. The fat little monster.

The front door opened. Mom came in, balancing a couple of bags of groceries.

"Hi, Mom!" I cried. I was glad she was home. Pam and Greg cooled it a little when she was around.

"Hi, honey." She carried the bags into the kitchen. "There's my little Biggie!" she cooed. "How's my sweet little pup?"

Everybody loves Biggie except for me.

"Greg!" Mom called. "It's your turn to make dinner tonight!"

"I can't!" Greg yelled from upstairs. "Mom — I've got so much homework to do! I can't fix dinner tonight."

Sure. He was so busy doing his homework, he couldn't stop driving me crazy.

"Make Matt do it," Pam shouted. "He's not doing anything. He's just watching TV."

"I have homework too, you know," I protested.

Greg came down the steps. "Right," he said. "Seventh-grade homework is *so* tough."

"I'll bet you didn't think it was easy when *you* were in seventh grade."

"Boys, please don't fight," Mom said. "I've only got a couple of hours before I have to go back to work. Matt, start dinner. I'm going to go upstairs and lie down for a few minutes."

I stormed into the kitchen. "Mom! It's not my turn!"

"Greg will cook another night," Mom promised.

"What about Pam?"

"Matt — that's enough. You're cooking. That's final." She dragged herself upstairs to her bedroom.

"Rats!" I muttered. I opened a cabinet door

and slammed it shut. "I never get my way around here!"

"What are you making for dinner, Matt?" Greg asked. "Geek burgers?"

"Matthew Amsterdam chews with his mouth open." Greg was talking into his stupid tape recorder again. We were all in the kitchen, eating dinner.

"Tonight the Amsterdams have tuna casserole for dinner," he said. "Matt defrosted it. He left it in the oven too long. The noodles on the bottom are burned."

"Shut up," I muttered.

Nobody said anything for a few minutes. The only sounds were forks clicking against plates and Biggie's toenails on the kitchen floor.

"How was school today, kids?" Mom asked.

"Mrs. Amsterdam asks her children about their day," Greg said to the tape recorder.

"Greg, do you have to do that at the dinner table?" Mom sighed.

"Mrs. Amsterdam complains about her son Greg's behavior," Greg murmured.

"Greg!"

"Greg's mother's voice gets louder. Could she be angry?"

"GREG!"

"I have to do it, Mom," Greg insisted in his normal voice. "It's for school!"

"It's getting on my nerves," Mom said.

"Mine too," I chimed in.

"Who asked you, Matt?" Greg snapped.

"So cut it out until after dinner, okay?" Mom asked.

Greg didn't say anything. But he set the tape recorder on the table and started to eat.

Pam said, "Mom, can I put my winter clothes in the closet in the guest room? My closet is packed."

"I'll think about it," Mom said.

"Hey!" I cried. "She has a huge closet! Her closet is almost as big as my whole room!"

"So?" Pam sneered.

"My room is the smallest one in the house!" I protested. "I can hardly walk through it."

"That's because you're a slob," Pam cracked.

"I'm not a slob! I'm neat! But I need a bigger bedroom. Mom, can I move into the guest room?"

Mom shook her head. "No."

"But why not?"

"I want to keep that room nice for guests," Mom explained.

"What guests?" I cried. "We never have any guests!"

"Your grandparents come every Christmas."

"That's once a year. Grandma and Grandpa won't mind sleeping in my little room once a year. The rest of the time they've got a whole house to themselves!"

11

"Your room is too small to sleep two people," Mom said. "I'm sorry, Matt. You can't have the guest room."

"Mom!"

"What do you care where you sleep, anyway?" Pam said. "You are the best sleeper in the world. You could sleep through a hurricane!"

Greg picked up the tape recorder. "When Matt isn't propped up in front of the TV, he is usually sleeping. He is asleep more than he's awake."

"Mom, Greg talked into the tape recorder again," I tattled.

"I know," Mom said wearily. "Greg, put it down."

"Mom, please let me switch rooms. I need a bigger room! I don't just sleep in my room — I *live* there! I need a place to get away from Pam and Greg. Mom — you don't know what it's like when you're not here! They're so mean to me!"

"Matt, stop it," Mom replied. "You have a wonderful brother and sister, and they take good care of you. You should appreciate them."

"I hate them!"

"Matt! I've had enough of this! Go to your room!"

"There's no room for me in there!" I cried.

"Now!"

As I ran upstairs to my room, I heard Greg say in his tape recorder voice, "Matt has been punished. His crime? Being a geek."

I slammed the door, stuffed my face in a pillow, and screamed.

I spent the rest of the evening in my room.

"It's not fair!" I muttered to myself. "Pam and Greg get whatever they want — and I get punished!"

Nobody is using the guest room, I thought. I don't care what Mom says. *I'm* sleeping there from now on.

Mom left for her night job. I waited until I heard Pam and Greg turn out the lights and go to their rooms. Then I slipped out of my room and into the guest room.

I was going to sleep in that guest room. And nothing was going to stop me.

I didn't think it was that big a deal. What was the worst thing that could happen? Mom might get mad at me. So what?

I had no idea that when I woke up in the morning, my life would be a complete disaster.

3

My feet were cold. That was the first thing I noticed when I woke up.

They were sticking out from under the covers. I sat up and tossed the blanket down over them.

Then I pulled the blanket back up. Were those *my* feet?

They were huge. Not monster huge, but huge for me. Way bigger than they'd been the day before.

Man, I thought. I'd heard about growth spurts. I knew kids grew fast at my age. But this was ridiculous!

I crept out of the guest room. I could hear Mom and Pam and Greg downstairs, eating breakfast.

Oh, no, I thought. I slept late. I hope no one noticed that I didn't sleep in my room last night.

I went to the bathroom to brush my teeth. Everything felt a little weird.

When I touched the bathroom doorknob, it

seemed to be in the wrong place. As if someone had lowered it during the night. The ceiling felt lower too.

I turned on the light and glanced in the mirror. Was that me?

I couldn't stop staring at myself. I looked like myself — and I didn't.

My face wasn't so round. I touched my upper lip. It was covered with blond fuzz. And I was about six inches taller than I'd been the day before!

I — I was *older*. I looked about sixteen years old!

No, no, I thought. This can't be right. I've got to be imagining this.

I'll just close my eyes for a minute. When I open them, I'll be twelve again.

I squeezed my eyes shut. I counted to ten.

I opened my eyes.

Nothing had changed.

I was a teenager!

My heart began to pound. I'd read that old story about Rip Van Winkle. He goes to sleep for a hundred years. When he wakes up, everything is different.

Did that happen to me? I wondered. Did I just sleep for four years straight?

I hurried downstairs to find Mom. She'd tell me what was going on.

15

I raced downstairs in my pajamas. I wasn't used to having such big feet. On the third step, I tripped over my left foot.

"Noooo!"

THUD!

I rolled the rest of the way down.

I landed on my face in front of the kitchen. Greg and Pam cracked up — of course.

"Nice one, Matt!" Greg said. "Ten points!"

I dragged myself to my feet. I had no time for Greg's jokes. I had to talk to Mom.

She sat at the kitchen table, eating eggs.

"Mom!" I cried. "Look at me!"

She looked at me. "I see you. You're not dressed yet. You'd better hurry or you'll be late for school."

"But, Mom!" I insisted. "I'm — I'm a teenager!"

"I'm all too aware of that," Mom said. "Now hurry up. I'm leaving in fifteen minutes."

"Yeah, hurry up, Matt," Pam piped up. "You'll make us late for school."

I turned to snap back at her — but stopped. She and Greg sat at the table, munching cereal.

Nothing weird about that, right?

The only thing was, they looked different too. If I was sixteen, Pam and Greg should have been nineteen and twenty.

But they weren't. They weren't even fifteen and sixteen.

They looked eleven and twelve!

They'd gotten younger!

"This is impossible!" I screeched.

"This is impossible!" Greg echoed, making fun of me.

Pam started giggling.

"Mom — listen to me!" I cried. "Something weird is going on. Yesterday I was twelve — and today I'm sixteen!"

"*You're* the weirdo!" Greg joked. He and Pam were cracking up. They were just as obnoxious now as they were when they were older.

Mom was only half-listening to me. I shook her arm to get her attention.

"Mom! Pam and Greg are my *older* brother and sister! But now suddenly they're younger! Don't you remember? Greg is the oldest!"

"Matt has gone cuckoo!" Greg cracked. "Cuckoo! Cuckoo!"

Pam fell on the floor laughing.

Mom stood up and set her plate in the sink. "Matt, I don't have time for this. Go upstairs and get dressed right now."

"But, Mom —"

"Now!"

What could I do? Nobody would listen to me. They all acted as if everything was normal.

I went upstairs and got dressed for school. I couldn't find my old clothes. My drawers were full of clothes I'd never seen before. They all fit my new, bigger body.

17

Could this be some kind of joke? I wondered as I laced up my size-ten sneakers.

Greg must be playing some crazy trick on me.

But how? How could Greg get me to grow — and get himself to shrink?

Even Greg couldn't do that.

Then Biggie trotted in.

"Oh, no," I cried. "Stay away, Biggie. Stay away!"

Biggie didn't listen. He ran right up to me — and licked me on the leg.

He didn't growl. He didn't bite. He wagged his tail.

That's it! I realized. Everything has really gone crazy.

"Matt! We're leaving!" Mom called.

I hurried downstairs and out the front door. Everybody else was already in the car.

Mom drove us to school. She pulled up in front of my school, Madison Middle School. I started to get out of the car.

"Matt!" Mom scolded. "Where are you going? Get back in here!"

"I'm going to school!" I explained. "I thought you wanted me to go to school!"

"Bye, Mom!" Pam chirped. She and Greg kissed Mom good-bye and hopped out of the car.

They ran into the school building.

"Stop fooling around, Matt," Mom said. "I'm going to be late for work."

18

I got back into the car. Mom drove another couple of miles. She stopped . . . in front of the high school.

"Here you are, Matt," Mom said.

I gulped. High school!

"But I'm not ready for high school!" I protested.

"What is your problem today?" Mom snapped. She reached across the front seat and opened my door. "Get going!"

I had to get out. I had no choice.

"Have a good day!" she called as she pulled away.

One look at that school and I knew — I was *not* going to have a good day.

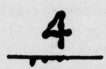

4

A bell rang. Big, scary-looking kids poured into the school building.

"Come on, kid. Let's move it." A teacher pushed me toward the door.

My stomach lurched. This was like the first day of school — times ten! Times a zillion!

I wanted to scream: I can't go to high school! I'm only in the seventh grade!

I wandered through the halls with hundreds of other kids. Where do I go? I wondered. I don't even know what class I'm in!

A big guy wearing a football jacket marched up to me and stuck his face in my face.

"Um, hello," I said. Who was this guy?

He didn't move. He didn't say a word. He just stood there, nose to nose with me.

"Um, listen," I began. "I don't know what class to go to. Do you know where they keep the kids who are about — you know — my age?"

The big — very, very big — guy opened his mouth.

"You little creep," he muttered. "I'm going to get you for what you did to me yesterday."

"Me?" My heart fluttered. What was he talking about? "*I* did something to *you*? I don't think so. I didn't do anything to you! I wasn't even here yesterday!"

He laid his huge paws on my shoulders — and squeezed.

"Ow!" I cried.

"Today, after school," he said slowly, "you're going to get it."

He let me go and walked slowly down the hall as if he owned the place.

I was so scared, I dove into the first classroom I came to.

I sat in the back. A tall woman with dark, curly hair stepped in front of the blackboard.

"All right, people!" she yelled. Everybody quieted down. "Open your books to page one fifty-seven."

What class is this? I wondered. I watched as the girl next to me pulled a textbook out of her bag. I looked at the cover.

No. Oh, no.

It couldn't be.

The title of the book was *Advanced Math: Calculus*.

Calculus! I'd never even heard of that!

I was bad at math — even seventh-grade math. How could I do calculus?

The teacher spotted me and narrowed her eyes. "Matt? Are you supposed to be in this class?"

"No!" I cried, jumping up from my seat. "I'm not supposed to be in this class, that's for sure!"

The teacher added, "You're in my two-thirty class, Matt. Unless you need to switch?"

"No, no! That's okay." I started backing out of the room. "I got mixed up, that's all!"

I hurried out of there as fast as I could. Close one, I thought. I won't be back at two-thirty, either.

I think I'll cut math class today.

Now what do I do? I wondered. I wandered down the hall. Another bell rang. Another teacher — a short, dumpy man with glasses — stepped into the hallway to close his classroom door. He spotted me.

"You're late again, Amsterdam," he barked at me. "Come on, come on."

I hurried into the classroom. I hoped this class would be something I could handle. Like maybe an English class where you read comic books.

No such luck.

It was an English class, all right.

But we weren't reading comic books. We were reading a book called *Anna Karenina*.

First of all, this book is about ten thousand

pages long. Second, everybody else had read it, and I hadn't. Third, even if I tried to read it, I wouldn't understand what was going on in a million years.

"Since you were the last one to class, Amsterdam," the teacher said, "you'll be the first to read. Start on page forty-seven."

I sat down at a desk and fumbled around. "Um, sir" — I didn't know the guy's name — "um — I don't have the book with me."

"No, of course you don't," the teacher sighed. "Robertson, would you please lend Amsterdam your book?"

Robertson turned out to be the girl sitting next to me. What was with this teacher, anyway? Calling everybody by their last names.

The girl passed her book to me. "Thanks, Robertson," I said. She scowled at me.

I guess she didn't like being called Robertson. But I didn't know her first name. I'd never seen her before in my life.

"Page forty-seven, Amsterdam," the teacher repeated.

I opened the book to page forty-seven. I scanned the page and took a deep breath.

That page was covered with big words. Hard words. Words I didn't know.

And then long Russian names.

I'm about to make a big fool of myself, I realized.

Just take it one sentence at a time, I told myself.

The trouble was, those sentences were long. One sentence took up the whole page!

"Are you going to read or aren't you?" the teacher demanded.

I took a deep breath and read the first sentence.

"'The young Princess Kitty Shcherb — Sherba — Sherbet —'"

Robertson snickered.

"*Shcherbatskaya*," the teacher corrected. "Not *Sherbet*. We've been over all these names, Amsterdam. You should know them by now."

Shcherbatskaya? Even after the teacher pronounced it for me, I couldn't say it. We never had words like that on our seventh-grade spelling tests.

"Robertson, take over for Amsterdam," the teacher commanded.

Robertson took her book back from me and started reading out loud. I tried to follow the story. It was something about people going to balls and some guys wanting to marry Princess Kitty. Girl stuff. I yawned.

"Bored, Amsterdam?" the teacher asked. "Maybe I can wake you up a bit. Why don't you tell us what this passage means?"

"Means?" I echoed. "You mean, what does it mean?"

"That's what I said."

I tried to stall for time. When would this stupid class be over, anyway?

"Um — mean? What does it mean," I murmured to myself, as if I were thinking really hard. "Like, what is the meaning of it? Wow, that's a tough one —"

All the other kids turned in their seats and stared at me.

The teacher tapped his foot. "We're waiting."

What could I do? I had no idea what was going on. I went for the foolproof escape.

"I have to go to the bathroom," I said.

Everybody laughed except the teacher. He rolled his eyes.

"Go ahead," he said. "And stop by the principal's office on your way back."

"What?"

"You heard me," the teacher said. "You've got a date with the principal. Now get out of my class."

I jumped up and ran out of the room. Man! High-school teachers were mean!

Even though I was being punished, I was glad to get out of there.

I never thought I'd say this, ever. But I wanted to go back to junior high! I wished everything would go back to normal.

I wandered through the hall, looking for the principal's office. I found a door with a frosted-glass window. Letters on the window said, MRS. McNAB, PRINCIPAL.

Should I go in? I wondered. Why should I? She's only going to yell at me.

I was about to turn around and leave. But someone was coming toward me down the hall.

Someone I didn't want to see.

"There you are, you little creep!" It was the big guy from this morning. "I'm going to pound your face into the ground!"

5

Gulp.

Suddenly the principal's office didn't seem so scary. This guy — whoever he was — would never hurt me in the principal's office.

"You'll be needing plastic surgery when I'm finished with you!" the guy yelled.

I opened the principal's door and slipped inside.

A big woman with steely gray hair sat behind a desk, writing something.

"Yes?" she said. "What is it?"

I paused to catch my breath. Why was I there again?

Oh, yeah. English class.

"My English teacher sent me," I explained. "I guess I'm in trouble."

"Sit down, Matt." She offered me a chair. She seemed kind of nice. She didn't raise her voice. "What's the problem?"

"There's been some kind of mistake," I began.

"I don't belong here. I'm not supposed to be in high school!"

She frowned. "What on earth are you talking about?"

"I'm twelve years old!" I cried. "I'm a seventh grader! I can't do this high school work. I'm supposed to be in middle school!"

She looked confused. She reached out and pressed the back of her hand to my forehead.

She's checking to see if I have a fever, I realized. I must sound like a maniac.

She spoke slowly and clearly. "Matt, you're in eleventh grade. Not seventh grade. Can you understand me?"

"I know I *look* like an eleventh grader," I said. "I can't do the work! Just now, in English class? They were reading a big, fat book called *Anna* something. I couldn't read the first sentence!"

"Calm down, Matt." She stood up and went to a file cabinet. "You *can* do the work. I'll prove it to you."

She pulled out a file and opened it. I stared at it. It was a school record, with grades and comments.

My name was written at the top of the chart. And there were my grades, for seventh grade, eighth grade, ninth grade, tenth grade, and the first half of eleventh.

"You see?" Mrs. McNab said. "You can do the work. You've gotten mostly B's, every year."

There were even a few A's.

"But — but I haven't *done* this yet," I protested. What was going on? How did I end up so far in the future? What happened to all those years?

"Mrs. McNab, you don't understand," I insisted. "Yesterday, I was twelve. Today I woke up — and I was sixteen! I mean, my body was sixteen. But my mind is still twelve!"

"Yes, I know," Mrs. McNab replied.

6

"Yes, I know you read a lot of science fiction," Mrs. McNab said. "But you don't expect me to believe that silly story — do you?"

Mrs. McNab folded her arms and sighed. I could tell she was losing patience with me.

"You have gym class next, don't you," she said.

"What?"

"This is all some kind of joke, right?" She glanced at my schedule, stapled to the file.

"I knew it," she muttered. "You *do* have gym next. And you're trying to get out of it."

"No! I'm telling the truth!"

"You're going to that gym class, young man," she said. "It starts in five minutes."

I stared at her. My feet felt glued to the floor. I should have known she wouldn't believe me.

"Are you going?" she asked gruffly. "Or do I have to take you to the gym myself?"

"I'm going, I'm going!" I backed out of the office and ran down the hall. Mrs. McNab stuck her head out the door and called, "No running in the halls!"

Pam and Greg always said that high school was bad, I thought as I trotted to the gym. But this is a nightmare!

Tweet! The gym teacher blew his whistle. "Volleyball! Line up to pick teams."

The gym teacher was a stocky guy with a black toupee. He chose a couple of team captains, and they started picking teams.

Don't pick me. Don't pick me, I silently prayed.

One of the captains, a blond girl named Lisa, picked me.

We lined up at the volleyball nets. The other team served. The ball flew at me like a bullet.

"I got it! I got it!" I cried.

I reached up to hit the ball back.

Klonk! It knocked me on the head.

"Ow!" I rubbed my sore head. I'd forgotten — my head was much higher now than it used to be.

"Wake up, Matt!" Lisa yelled.

I had a feeling I wasn't going to be very good at volleyball.

The ball came flying at us again. "Get it, Matt!" someone called.

I reached up higher this time. But I tripped over my giant feet and fell — *oof!* — on top of the guy standing next to me.

"Watch it, man!" the guy shouted. "Get off

me!" Then he clutched his elbow. "Ow! I hurt my elbow!"

The teacher blew his whistle and hurried over to the guy. "You'd better go to the nurse," he said.

The guy hobbled out of the gym.

"Way to go, Matt," Lisa said sarcastically. "Try to do something right this time, okay?"

I turned red with embarrassment. I knew I looked like a jerk. But I wasn't used to being so tall! And having such big feet and hands. I didn't know how to control them.

I got through a few rounds without messing up. Actually, the ball didn't come near me. So I didn't have the chance to mess up. Then Lisa said, "Your serve, Matt."

I knew this was coming. I'd been watching everybody else serve so I'd know what to do.

This time I won't mess up, I vowed. I'm going to serve this ball and get a point for my team. Then they won't be angry at me for making us lose.

I tossed the ball in the air. I punched it as hard as I could with my fist, trying to get it over the net.

WHAM! I hit that ball harder than I'd ever hit anything. It whizzed through the air so fast, you could hardly see it.

SMACK!

"Ow!"

Lisa doubled over, clutching the side of her head.

"Why did you have to hit it so hard?" Lisa cried, rubbing her head.

The teacher looked her over. "You'll have a nasty bruise there," he said. "You'd better go to the nurse too."

Lisa glared at me and stumbled away.

The teacher gave me a funny look. "What's the matter, kid?" he asked. "Don't know your own strength? Or just out to get your classmates, one by one?"

"I — I didn't do it on purpose," I stuttered. "I swear I didn't!"

"Hit the showers, kid," the teacher said.

I hung my head as I dragged myself to the locker room.

This day can't get any worse, I thought. There's no way.

Still, why take chances?

It was lunchtime. I had half a day of school to go.

But I wasn't going to stick around.

I didn't know where to go or what to do. I only knew I couldn't stay in that school.

High school was horrible. If I ever got back to my normal life, I'd remember to skip this part.

I left the gym and raced out of the school building as fast as I could. Down the hall. Out the door.

I glanced back. Was that big guy chasing me? Did the principal see me sneak out?

No sign of anyone. Coast clear.

Then — *oof!*

Oh, no. Not again!

7

I bumped into someone. I bounced backwards and landed with a thud on the ground.

Ow! What happened?

A girl sat sprawled on the sidewalk. Books were scattered around her.

I helped her up. "Are you okay?" I asked.

She nodded.

"I'm really sorry," I said. "I've been doing that all day."

"That's all right." The girl smiled. "I'm not hurt."

She wasn't a high-school girl — she looked about my age. I mean, the age I thought I was. Which was twelve.

She was pretty, with long, thick blond hair in a ponytail. Her blue eyes sparkled at me.

She bent down to pick up her stuff.

"I'll help you," I offered. I reached down to pick up a book.

CLONK! My head bumped into hers.

"I did it again!" I cried. I was getting sick of this.

"Don't worry about it," the girl said. She picked up the rest of the books.

"My name is Lacie," she told me.

"I'm Matt."

"What's the matter, Matt?" she asked. "Why are you in such a hurry?"

What could I tell her? That my whole life had turned inside out?

Then the school door burst open. Mrs. McNab stepped outside.

"I've got to get out of here," I replied. "I've got to get home. See you."

I ran down the street before Mrs. McNab could spot me.

I collapsed on the couch. It had been a terrible day. At least I made it home before that big guy beat me up.

But what was I going to do tomorrow?

I watched TV until Pam and Greg came home from school.

Pam and Greg. I'd forgotten all about them.

They were little kids now. And they seemed to expect me to take care of them.

"Fix us a snack! Fix us a snack!" Pam chanted.

"Fix your own snack," I snapped back.

"I'm telling Mommy!" Pam cried. "You're supposed to fix us a snack! And I'm hungry!"

I remembered the excuse Pam and Greg had always used to get out of doing stuff for me.

"I've got homework to do," I said.

Oh, yeah, I realized.

I probably really *do* have homework to do.

High-school homework.

It's going to be impossible for me.

But if I don't do it, I'll be in trouble tomorrow.

In more ways than one, I thought, remembering that big guy. What did I ever do to him, anyway?

When it was time for bed, I headed to my old room. But Pam was sleeping in there.

So I went back to the guest room. I climbed into bed.

What am I going to do? I worried as I let my eyes close.

I don't know what's happening.

I can't do anything right.

Is this what my life is going to be like — forever?

8

I opened my eyes. Sunlight poured in through the window. It was morning.

Oh, great, I thought. Time for another fabulous day of high school.

I shut my eyes again. I can't face it, I thought. Maybe if I stay in bed, all my problems will go away.

"Matt! Time to get up!" Mom called.

I sighed. Mom would never let me stay home from school. There was no way out.

"Matt!" she shouted again.

Her voice sounds funny, I thought. Higher than usual.

Maybe she's not so tired for once.

I dragged myself out of bed. I set my feet on the floor.

Wait a minute.

My feet.

I stared at them. They looked different. I mean, they looked the same.

They weren't big anymore. I had my old feet back!

I looked at my hands. I wiggled my fingers.

It was me! I was my old self again!

I ran into the bathroom to check the mirror. I had to make sure.

I flipped on the light.

There I was — a puny little twelve year old!

I hopped up and down. "Yippee! I'm twelve! I'm twelve!"

All my problems were solved! I didn't have to go to high school!

I didn't have to face that big bully!

The nightmare was over!

Everything was okay now. I was even looking forward to seeing Pam and Greg and Biggie as their crabby old selves again.

"Matt! You're going to be late!" Mom shouted.

Does she have a cold or something? I wondered as I quickly dressed and ran downstairs. She really did sound different.

I practically skipped into the kitchen. "I'll have cereal today, Mom —"

I stopped.

Two people sat at the kitchen table. A man and a woman.

I'd never seen them before.

9

"I fixed you some toast, Matt," the woman said.

"Where's my mother?" I asked. "Where are Pam and Greg?"

The man and woman stared blankly at me.

"Feeling a little off today, son?" the man said.

Son?

The woman stood up and bustled around the kitchen. "Drink your juice, honey. Your dad will drop you off at school today."

My dad?

"I don't have a dad!" I insisted. "My father has been dead since I was a baby!"

The man shook his head and bit into a piece of toast. "They told me he'd get weird at this age. But I didn't know *how* weird."

"Where are they?" I demanded. "What did you do with my family?"

"I'm not in the mood for jokes today, Matt," the man said. "Now let's get moving."

A cat crept into the kitchen. It rubbed against my legs.

"What's this cat doing here?" I asked. "Where's Biggie?"

"Who's Biggie? What are you talking about?" the woman said.

I was starting to get scared. My heart was pounding. My legs felt weak.

I sank into a chair and gulped my juice. "Are you saying that — you're my parents?"

The woman kissed me on the head. "I'm your mother. This is your father. That's your cat. Period."

"I have no brothers or sisters?"

The woman raised an eyebrow and glanced at the man. "Brothers and sisters? No, darling."

I cringed. My real mother would never call me "darling."

"I know you want a brother," the woman went on. "But you really wouldn't like it. You're just not good at sharing."

I couldn't stand this any longer.

"Okay, stop right there," I demanded. "Stop fooling around. I want to know right now — why is this happening to me?"

My "parents" exchanged looks. Then they turned back to me.

"I want to know who you are!" I cried, trembling all over. "Where is my real family? I want answers — now!"

The man stood up and grabbed me by the arm. "Get in the car, son," he commanded.

"No!" I screamed.

"Joke is over. Now get in the car."

I had no choice. I followed him to a car — a shiny new one, not my real mother's old piece of junk. I climbed in.

The woman ran outside. "Don't forget your books!" she called. She pushed a backpack through the open window at me. Then she kissed me again.

"Ugh!" I cringed. "Stop it!" I didn't know her well enough to let her kiss me.

The man started the car and pulled out of the driveway. The woman waved. "Have a good day at school!"

They're serious, I realized. They really think they're my parents.

I shuddered.

What was happening to me?

10

One day I'm a normal twelve year old. The next day I'm suddenly sixteen.

Then the next day I'm twelve again — except I live in a completely different family!

I stared out the window as "Dad" drove. We passed through a neighborhood I'd never seen before.

"Where are we going?" I asked in a tiny voice.

"I'm taking you to school. What did you think — we were going to the circus?" the man replied.

"This isn't the way to school," I said.

The man just snorted and shook his head. He didn't believe me.

He pulled up in front of a junior high school — but not mine. I'd never seen this place before.

"Okay, son. Have a nice day." The man reached across me and opened the car door.

What could I do? I climbed out of the car.

"Dad" drove off.

Now what? I thought. I'm twelve again — but I'm at a totally different school.

Am I awake?

I kicked myself in the shin to test it. Ow! That hurt.

I figured that meant I was awake.

Kids poured into the school building. I followed them in. I didn't know what else to do.

Ahead of me I saw a girl with a long, thick blond ponytail. She turned around and smiled at me.

She looked familiar. Where had I seen her before?

"Hi," I said to her.

"Hi," she said back. Her blue eyes sparkled at me.

"I'm Matt." I was still racking my brains trying to figure out where I'd met her before.

"I'm Lacie."

Lacie! Of course. I'd crashed into her the day before — outside Horrible High.

I started to say, "I met you yesterday — remember?" But I stopped.

Did she recognize me? I couldn't tell. But why should she? I looked completely different from the day before. How could she guess that the twelve-year-old kid standing next to her was also the clumsy teenager from yesterday?

"What's your first class?" she asked me. "I've got lunch."

"Lunch? But it's eight-thirty in the morning!"

"You're new here, aren't you?" she said.

I nodded.

"This stupid school is so crowded, they can't fit everyone into the cafeteria at lunchtime," she explained. "So I've got lunch now."

"I've got lunch too," I lied. Or maybe it wasn't a lie — what did I know? I had no idea what was going on anymore. School was beginning to seem like a lot more trouble than it was worth.

I followed her to the cafeteria. They really were serving lunch there. The powerful smell of brussels sprouts stank up the air. I gagged.

"It's too early in the morning for brussels sprouts," I noted.

"Let's eat out on the playground," Lacie suggested. "It's a nice day."

We slipped out of the cafeteria and settled under a tree. Lacie sipped a carton of chocolate milk. I rummaged through my backpack for some lunch. I figured my new "mom" must've packed me something.

She did, all right. Baloney and ketchup on white bread. A little plastic bag full of carrot sticks. Vanilla pudding for dessert.

Everything I hate.

Lacie held out a chocolate cupcake. "Want this? I can't face it this early in the morning."

"Thanks." I took the cupcake.

Lacie seemed like a really nice person. She was

the nicest person I'd met since my life became a nightmare. She was the *only* nice person I'd met since then.

Maybe she would understand. I really wanted to talk to somebody. I felt so alone.

"Do I look familiar to you?" I asked her.

She studied my face.

"You do look kind of familiar," she said. "I'm sure I've seen you around school. . . ."

"That's not what I mean." I decided to tell her what had happened to me. I knew it would sound weird to her. But I had to tell somebody.

I started slowly. "Were you walking past the high school yesterday?"

"Yes. I walk past it every day on my way home."

"Did someone bump into you yesterday? A teenager? In front of the high school?"

She started to answer. But something caught her eye. I followed her gaze to the school door.

Two guys were walking toward us. They were tough-looking guys in black jeans and black T-shirts. One wore a blue bandanna around his head. The other had ripped the sleeves of his T-shirt to show off his beefy arms.

They had to be at least sixteen or seventeen. What were they doing here?

They headed straight for us.

My heart began to pound. Something told me to be afraid of them.

Maybe it was the nasty looks on their faces.

"Who are those guys?" I asked.

Lacie didn't answer. She didn't have time.

One of the guys in black pointed at me.

"There he is!" he shouted.

"Get him!"

11

The two guys ran straight for me.

Who were they? I didn't know.

But I didn't stop to think. I jumped to my feet and ran as fast as I could.

I glanced back. Were they chasing me?

"Stop him!" one of them shouted.

Lacie stepped in front of them, blocking their path.

"Thanks, Lacie," I whispered. I hurried out of the playground. I raced through the strange neighborhood, trying to remember how to get home.

A few blocks from school I stopped to catch my breath.

No sign of the two guys. No sign of Lacie, either.

I hope she's all right, I thought. They didn't seem to want to hurt her.

They wanted to hurt *me*.

But why?

The day before, a bully had said he wanted to get me after school.

But today, in my new, weird world, I hadn't seen him. Neither of the guys in black was that bully.

Just two *new* bullies.

I've got to get help, I realized.

I don't know what's happening. But it's all too much for me. And it's too frightening. I hardly know who I am.

I drifted through the streets until I finally found my way home. "Mom" and "Dad" were out. The front door was locked. I climbed in through the kitchen window.

My real mother was gone. My brother and sister and even my dog were gone.

But there must be someone else I know, I thought. Somebody, somewhere, who can help me.

Maybe my real mom went somewhere else. Maybe she's visiting relatives or something.

I decided to try Aunt Margaret and Uncle Andy. I dialed Aunt Margaret's number.

A man answered the phone.

"Uncle Andy!" I cried. "It's me, Matt!"

The voice said, "Who is this?"

"Matt!" I repeated. "Your nephew!"

"I don't know any Matt," the man said gruffly. "You must have dialed the wrong number."

"No — Uncle Andy, wait!" I shouted.

"My name isn't Andy," the man snarled. He hung up.

I stared at the phone, stunned. The man didn't sound like Uncle Andy at all.

I guess I *did* dial wrong, I thought. I tried the number again.

"Hello?" It was the same man again.

This time I tried a new approach. "Is Andy Amsterdam there, please?"

"You again! There's no Andy here, kid," the man said. "Wrong number."

He slammed the phone in my ear.

I tried not to panic. But my hands were shaking.

I dialed information. "What listing, please?" the operator asked.

"Andrew Amsterdam," I said.

"Checking," said the operator.

A minute later she said, "I'm sorry. We have no listing under that name."

"Maybe if I spell it for you," I insisted. "A-m-s —"

"I've already checked, sir. There's no one listed under that name."

"Could you try Margaret Amsterdam, then?"

"There's no one named Amsterdam listed at all, sir."

My heart started racing as I hung up. This

can't be happening, I thought. There must be somebody I know, somewhere!

I won't give up. I'll try my cousin Chris.

I called Chris's number. Someone else answered.

It was as if Chris didn't exist. Or Uncle Andy, or my mother, or anybody I knew.

How could my whole family disappear?

The only person I knew was Lacie. But I couldn't call her.

I didn't know her last name.

The front door opened. The woman who called herself my mother bustled in, carrying shopping bags.

"Matt, darling! What are you doing home in the middle of the day?"

"None of your beeswax," I snapped.

"Matt! Don't be so rude!" she scolded.

I shouldn't have been rude to her, I guess. But what difference did it make? She wasn't my real mother, anyway.

My real mother had disappeared off the face of the earth.

I shuddered. I realized I was totally alone in the world.

I didn't know anyone — not even my parents!

12

"Bedtime, honey," my fake mother chirped.

I'd been sitting in front of the TV all evening. Just staring, not even really watching it.

Maybe I should stop thinking of these people as my fake parents, I realized. They're real enough now. I might be stuck with them forever.

I'll find out in the morning, I thought as I trudged upstairs. My old room was a sewing room now. I went back to the guest room to sleep.

"Good night, darling." "Mom" kissed me goodnight. Why did she have to keep kissing me?

She turned out the light and said, "See you in the morning."

The morning. I dreaded the morning.

So far, each morning was weirder than the last. I was scared to go to sleep.

What would I wake up to?

It would be great if these fake parents of mine were gone. But who would take their place?

Maybe I'd wake up and the whole world would be gone!

I struggled to stay awake. Please, I prayed. Please let everything be normal again. I'd even be glad to have Greg and Pam back, if everything could only be normal. . . .

I must have fallen asleep. The next thing I knew, I opened my eyes — and it was morning.

I lay perfectly still for a minute. Had anything changed?

I heard noises in the house. There were definitely other people here.

A *lot* of other people.

My heart started pounding. Oh, no, I thought. What am I in for this time?

I heard someone playing an accordion. That was a pretty sure sign my old family wasn't back.

But first things first. How old was I today?

I held my hands up in front of my face. They looked a little on the small side.

I got up and went to the bathroom, trying not to panic. I was really getting sick of this routine.

The mirror seemed higher than usual. I stared at my face.

I wasn't twelve anymore, that was for sure. I looked about eight.

Eight, I thought, sighing.

That's third grade. Well, at least I'll be able to do the math.

Suddenly, I felt a sharp pain in my back.

Ow! Claws! Tiny claws digging into my back! The claws dug deeper.

I screamed.

13

Something jumped on my back!

A tiny, hairy face appeared in the mirror. Some kind of animal was standing on my shoulders!

"Get it off! Get it off!" I shrieked.

"Eeee! Eeee!" the animal screeched.

I ran into the hallway — and almost crashed into a huge man.

"Get this thing off me!" I cried.

The man plucked the animal off my shoulder. He laughed loud and deep, like an evil Santa Claus.

"What's wrong with you, Matt?" he boomed. "Scared of Pansy all of a sudden?"

Pansy? The man cuddled the animal in his arms. It was a monkey.

The man roughed up my hair. "Get dressed, boy. We got a rehearsal this morning."

Rehearsal? What was that supposed to mean?

I stared at the man. He was huge, with a round stomach, glossy black hair, and a long mustache.

The weirdest part was what he wore: a bright red costume with gold trim and a gold belt.

Oh, no! I thought, my heart sinking. This can't be . . . my father?

From downstairs a woman's voice screamed, "Grub!"

The man handed me a pile of clothes. "Put your costume on," he said. "Then come on down to breakfast — son."

I knew it. He *was* my father. For today, at least. My "family" kept getting worse every day.

"GRUUUUB!" the woman downstairs yelled again.

I guess that's Mom, I thought miserably. She sounds like a real sweetheart.

Kids came pouring out of the other bedrooms. It seemed like there were dozens of them, all different ages. But I counted, and there were only six.

I tried to get all the new facts straight. I was eight years old. I had six brothers and sisters and a pet monkey. I hadn't seen my mother yet, but my father was a total wacko.

And I've got to wear some kind of freaky costume, I thought, holding up the clothes the man had given me. It was a tight blue outfit, like a leotard. The bottom part was blue with white stripes. The top had white stars.

What was that supposed to be? And what kind of rehearsal did I have?

Was I in a play or something?

I pulled on the costume. It fit me like a second skin. I felt like a total jerk.

Then I went downstairs for breakfast.

The kitchen was a madhouse. The other kids laughed and shouted and threw food. Pansy hopped around on the table, stealing bits of bacon.

A tall, thin woman piled pancakes on plates. She wore a long, purple, sequined gown. A silver crown perched on top of her head.

My new mom.

"Hurry up and eat, Matt — before it's all gone!" she shouted.

I grabbed a plate and started eating. I had to keep swatting Pansy away.

"Doesn't Matt look cute in his little superhero suit?" a girl teased. She had to be one of my older sisters.

"Cute as a button," a boy said sarcastically. He looked about two years older than me. He grabbed my cheek and pinched it — hard. Too hard. "Cute little Matt," he sneered. "Big-shot star of the circus."

The circus! I dropped my fork. Chills rippled down my back. Was I in the circus?

The dopey costumes. The monkey. It all made sense now.

I dropped my head into my hands. Matthew Amsterdam, circus boy. I almost wanted to cry.

I had the feeling my brother was jealous. As if *he* wanted to be the star of the stupid circus.

And he could be, for all I cared. *I* sure didn't want to be the star of any circus.

"Leave Matt alone or he'll get stage fright again," the mother scolded.

I studied the rest of the family. Everyone was dressed in bright costumes. I was part of a circus family.

The pancakes sank to the pit of my stomach. I never liked the circus. Even when I was little, I hated it.

But now the circus was my life — and I was the star. Oh, goody.

"Rehearsal time!" the father cried. He put a black top hat on his head and cracked a whip on the stairs. "Let's roll!"

We left our plates on the table and piled into a beat-up old van. Mom drove at about ninety miles an hour.

My brothers and sisters fought the whole way. One little girl kept pinching me. Another one punched me.

"Cut it out!" I snapped. Why couldn't I wake up in a world with *nice* brothers and sisters?

The van chugged into a fairground and stopped in front of a big circus tent.

"Everybody out!" Dad ordered.

I jostled with my brothers and sisters to get

out of the van. Then I followed them into the tent.

It was kind of awesome inside the tent. Other acts were already there, practicing. I saw a man on a high wire way up near the top of the tent. An elephant stood up on its hind legs and danced. Clowns rode around in dopey little cars, honking their horns.

I wonder what *my* act is? I thought. Two of my sisters scurried up a ladder and started practicing a trapeze routine.

I watched them, terrified. The trapeze! There was *no way* they could get me up there. *No way*.

Please don't make me do a trapeze act, I prayed.

"Come on, Matt," Dad said. "Let's get to work."

Not the trapeze. Not the trapeze, I prayed.

Dad led me away from the trapeze ladder. I began to relax. Whatever I had to do, it couldn't be worse than swinging around on a trapeze. Right?

Wrong.

Dad led me to the back of the tent. I followed him through a maze of animal cages.

Dad strode up to one of the cages and opened the door.

"All right, son," he bellowed. "Get in."

My jaw dropped. I couldn't believe my ears.

"G-g-g-get in?" I stuttered. "But — there's a *lion* in that cage!"

The lion opened his huge jaws and roared. I backed away, shivering.

"Are you going to walk in?" Dad prodded me with the end of his whip. "Or do I have to push you?"

I didn't move. I couldn't.

So Dad pushed me into the lion's cage — and shut the door.

14

I backed up against the cage wall. The cold steel bars pressed into my back. My legs were trembling so hard, I thought I would fall on my face.

The lion stared at me. He sniffed the air.

I've heard that animals can smell fear. This lion got a noseful.

My "father" — the lion tamer — stood beside me in the cage.

"We're trying a new trick today, Matt," he said. "You're going to ride the lion."

He might as well have punched me in the stomach. I was going to ride the lion?

Yeah. Right.

Some father this guy is, I thought. Feeding his own son to a lion.

The lion stood up. I kept my eyes on him. My whole body shook with fear.

ROOOAAAR!

The lion's breath blew in my face like a hot wind. My hair stood on end.

The lion stepped toward us. Dad cracked his whip. "Ha!" he shouted.

The lion stepped back, licking his chops.

"Go on, boy," Dad boomed at me. "Climb on Hercules's back. Then slide up to his shoulders. I'll crack the whip to make him walk around the cage."

I couldn't say a word. I just stared at the man in total disbelief.

"Why are you looking at me like that? You're not afraid of Hercules, are you?"

"A-afraid?" I stammered. "Afraid" wasn't the word. *Petrified*, maybe. Terrified, horrified, frozen with fear. But afraid? Nah.

He cracked his whip again. "No son of mine is a coward!" he shouted. "You get on that lion's back — NOW!"

Then he leaned down and whispered, "Just watch that he doesn't bite you. Remember your poor brother Tom. He's still trying to learn how to write left-handed."

He cracked the whip again — right at my feet.

I wasn't going to ride the lion. No way.

And I couldn't stay in that cage another second.

Dad cracked his whip at me again. I jumped.

"Noooo!" I shrieked.

I tugged the cage door open. I ran out of that cage so fast, Dad hardly knew what happened.

I raced out of the tent. My brain screamed, "Hide! Find a hiding place — quick!"

I spotted a couple of trailers in the parking lot. I darted behind one — and bumped right into Lacie.

"You again!" I gasped. It was weird how she kept popping up.

"I've got to hide," I told her. "I'm in trouble!"

"What's wrong, Matt?" she asked.

"I'm about to become lion food!" I cried. "Help me!"

Lacie yanked on the trailer door. It was locked.

"Oh, no!" I groaned. "Look!"

I pointed past the trailer. Two guys were running toward us.

I'd seen them before. The two guys in black.

They were coming after me!

I ran. There was no place to go, no place to hide — except back inside the tent.

I burst through the tent flap. I tried to catch my breath while my eyes adjusted to the dark.

I heard one of the guys in black shout, "In there! He went inside the tent!"

I stumbled through the darkness, searching for a place to hide.

"Get him!" The boys were inside the tent now.

I ran blindly — right back into the lion's cage.

15

I slammed the cage door shut. The guys in black gripped the steel bars and shook them.

"You won't get away!" one shouted.

My "dad," the lion tamer, was gone. I was alone in the cage — with Hercules.

"Easy, boy. Easy . . ." I murmured as I inched my way along the side of the cage. The lion stood in the center, eyeing me.

The two guys rattled the cage door again. It swung open. They stepped inside, glaring at me.

"You can't escape that easily," one of them warned.

The lion growled at them. "It's just an old circus lion," one guy said. "He won't hurt us."

But I could tell they weren't as sure as they sounded.

Hercules growled again, louder this time. The two guys stopped.

I inched farther around the cage wall.

I had to put that lion between me and the guys in black. It was my only chance.

Carefully, one of the guys stepped forward. The lion roared at him.

He stepped back.

The lion's eyes darted from the guys to me and back. I knew he was trying to decide who would make the tastier meal.

"You'd better get out of here," I warned. "Hercules hasn't been fed yet."

The guys watched Hercules warily.

"He won't attack me," I bluffed. "I'm his master. But if I tell him to, he'll go right for your throats!"

The guys glanced at each other. One of them said, "He's lying."

The other guy didn't look so sure.

"I'm not lying," I insisted. "Get out of here right now — or I'll turn him on you!"

One guy made a move for the cage door. The other guy grabbed his arm and pulled him back. "Don't be chicken," he snapped.

"Get them, Hercules!" I shouted. "Get them!"

Hercules let out his fiercest roar yet — and pounced.

The guys in black scurried out of the cage. They slammed the door as Hercules tried to bound out.

"You won't get away!" one guy yelled through the bars. "We'll be back!"

"Why do you want me?" I screamed after them. "What did I do? What did I do?"

16

Hercules didn't really want to eat anybody. He just wanted to get out of the cage.

He didn't try to stop me as I slipped out. I sneaked away to hide in the van until circus practice was over.

"Where were you all day?" Dad grumbled when he found me. Everyone else piled into the van, and we drove home.

"I felt sick," I complained. "I had to lie down."

"You're going to learn that trick tomorrow, Matt," Dad insisted. "You *won't* get out of it again."

I just yawned. I figured tomorrow would never come. At least not for my circus family.

Tomorrow would bring some new horror. Or maybe for once something good would happen.

I went to bed early that night. I didn't like being an eight year old in a circus family. I couldn't wait for it to be over.

My circus brothers were climbing the walls in

my old room. I'd never get any sleep in there. So I crept off to sleep in the guest room again.

But I had trouble falling asleep. I couldn't stop wondering what the next day would bring. It's hard to relax when you don't know what kind of world you'll wake up to in the morning.

I tried counting sheep, but that never works for me. So I tried to think of all the good things that could happen when I woke up.

I could wake up as a major league baseball player. I could be the greatest pitcher in the history of baseball.

Or I could be a very, very rich kid who gets everything he wants.

Or I could be a space explorer five hundred years in the future.

Why didn't anything like *that* ever happen to me?

Most of all, I wished I could wake up and find my family again. My *real* family. They drove me crazy. But at least I was used to them. I even missed them, a little bit.

Okay, a *lot*.

At last, just before dawn, I fell asleep.

It was still very early when I woke up. I gazed around the room. Everything seemed a little blurry.

Who am I now? I wondered. The room looked

normal. I didn't hear any noise, so I knew the circus family was gone.

Might as well get it over with, I decided. I jumped out of bed. I felt a little shaky on my legs.

I walked slowly into the bathroom. I looked in the mirror.

No. Oh, no.

This was the worst one yet. The worst ever. The worst *possible*!

17

I was an old man!

"No!" I screamed. I couldn't take it anymore. I ran back to bed as fast as my rickety old legs would carry me.

I got under the covers and closed my eyes. I was going right back to sleep. I wasn't about to spend the whole day as an old man. Not when I'm really only twelve.

I quickly dozed off. When I woke up, I knew right away I had changed. I wasn't an old man anymore.

I felt a surge of energy. Power. I felt strong.

Maybe I'm a baseball player after all, I thought hopefully.

I rubbed my eyes. That's when I caught a glimpse of my hand.

It — it was *green*. My skin was green. And instead of fingers, I had claws!

I swallowed hard. I tried to shake away my panic.

What had happened to me this time?

I didn't waste a second finding out. I lumbered to the bathroom mirror.

When I saw my face, I let out a roar of horror and disgust.

I had become a monster. A hideous, gross monster.

18

I tried to scream. I tried to shout, "This can't be happening to me!"

But all that came out was a terrifying snarl.

No! I thought, in a total panic. I felt like tearing my horrible skin off. I was a hideous monster — and I couldn't even talk!

I was big — almost seven feet tall — and powerful. My skin was a scaly green with black stripes, like a lizard. I oozed slime all over.

My head looked like a dinosaur's, with warts all over it. Three spiky horns stuck out of the top of my head, between four pointy ears.

My hands and feet had sharp claws. My toenails clicked on the bathroom floor when I walked.

I was one ugly, ugly dude.

I wished I'd stayed an old man. Each time I woke up, my life got worse! When was this ever going to end? How could I make it stop?

I thought about Lacie. She seemed to pop up no matter where I went.

And she had tried to help me escape from those guys in black, I remembered. She wants to help me.

I've got to find her, I decided. I know she's out there somewhere.

She's my only chance.

I staggered through the house in my monster body. The house was empty. At least I didn't have a family to deal with. A family full of monsters would have been a *real* nightmare!

I had to be grateful for the little things. Especially when I had green skin and spikes growing out of my head.

I lumbered out the door and down the street. I tried to shout, "Lacie! Lacie, where are you!"

But my mouth couldn't make the words. All that came out was a booming, terrifying roar.

A car driving down the street stopped suddenly. The driver gaped at me through the windshield.

"Don't be afraid!" I cried. But that's not what came out. Another roar ripped through the air.

The man screamed and backed his car down the street at full speed. He crashed into another car.

I went over to see if anyone was hurt. A woman and her kid were in the other car.

They must have been all right. Because as soon as they saw me, they all jumped out of their cars and ran away, screaming their heads off.

My giant lizard feet carried me to the center of town. I smashed through bushes, kicked garbage cans over. People screamed in terror as soon as they saw me.

Lacie, I thought. I've got to find Lacie.

I tried to keep this thought in my head. But I was getting hungry. Very, very hungry.

Normally I like peanut butter and jelly for a snack. But that day I had a strong craving for metal. A nice, big, crunchy hunk of metal.

The town was in a panic. People raced around, shrieking as if it were the end of the world.

But I wasn't going to hurt anybody. All I wanted was a little snack.

I stepped in front of a tasty-looking compact car. The driver slammed on the brakes.

ROOAARR! I beat my chest with my powerful monster arms.

The driver cowered in the car. I reached out and snatched off a windshield wiper. Just for a taste.

Mmmmm. Rubbery goodness.

The man flung the car door open. "No!" he cried. "Don't hurt me! L-leave me alone!"

He ran away to hide somewhere. It was nice of him to leave me his car.

I ripped the door off the car. I pulled the handle off and stuffed it into my mouth.

Delicious. Nice cool chrome.

Then I took a big bite out of the door. Chomp, chomp. My teeth were huge and sharp as a razor — they had no trouble chewing the metal. Yum — leather upholstery for extra flavor. I finished off the door and reached in to rip out a bucket seat.

Bits of yellow foam rubber spewed out of my mouth as I ate. The leather was yummy. But the foam padding was kind of dry. It was like air-popped popcorn with no butter. Bleh.

I was tearing out the steering wheel when I heard sirens.

Uh-oh.

I saw that a mob had gathered around me. People pointed at me.

"It's eating a car!" someone screeched.

Well, duhhh, I thought. What do you expect a monster to eat — Rice Krispies?

The sirens came closer. Police cars were pulling up all around me.

"Clear the way," came a voice over a loudspeaker. "Stand back. Clear the way."

I'd better get out of here, I decided. I dropped the steering wheel I was nibbling and began to run. People screamed and scattered out of the way.

"Stop it! Get the monster!"

The squeal of police sirens ripped through the air. If they caught me, I knew they'd try to lock me up — or worse.

I had to get out of there. I had to hide.

I stumbled through the crowds. I headed for the edge of town.

Then I spotted her. Lacie. Mobs of people were running away from me. She was the only one running *toward* me.

I snarled, trying to call Lacie. She grabbed me by my slimy arm and pulled me out of the crowd.

She led me down an alley. We lost the mob. I wanted to ask her where we were going. But I knew the words wouldn't come. I was afraid a roar might scare her.

We ran and ran. We didn't stop running until we reached the woods at the edge of town. Lacie pulled me into the woods, deeper and deeper.

She's hiding me, I thought gratefully. I wished I could thank her.

I followed Lacie down a narrow path. Then the path ended. We pushed our way through the brush.

At last we came to a small house. It was well hidden by trees and vines. You could hardly see it, even when you stood right in front of it.

A hideout, I thought. How did Lacie find this place?

I wondered if there was anything good to eat inside the house. I was getting hungry again.

A couple of bicycles would taste good right now, I thought.

Lacie opened the door of the house. She beckoned me to come inside.

I went in. Two people stepped out of the shadows.

No. Oh, no.

Not them.

But it *was* them.

The guys in black.

One of them spoke.

"Thank you for bringing him to us," he said. "You did your job well."

19

RRRROOOOOOAAAAARRRR!

I thrashed my arms. I was furious!

Lacie betrayed me!

I had to get out of there — fast.

I dove for the door — but they dropped a net over me.

They yanked on the net — and I tripped.

I fell with a heavy thud. The two guys closed the net over me.

I roared and thrashed with all my might. But I couldn't get out. They tied the net tightly around me.

"Get me out of here!" I wanted to scream. I slashed at the net with my claws. I bit it with my teeth. But it was made of some kind of strange material. I couldn't break the strings.

I snarled and kicked for a long time. But no matter what I did, I was still trapped. At last I got tired. I lay on my back on the floor.

Lacie and the two guys in black stared down at me, perfectly calm.

I wished I could talk. I couldn't stop myself from trying.

"How could you do this to me?" I tried to ask Lacie. "I thought you were my friend!"

Nothing but snarls and growls came out of me. Lacie stared down at me. She couldn't understand what I said.

The guys in black just folded their arms across their chests and sneered at me.

"Who are you?" I wanted to ask them. "What do you want? What is happening to me?"

No one answered me. One of the guys, the taller one, said, "All right. Let's lock him up in the back."

I roared again. I struggled as the three of them dragged my big, slimy body across the floor. They pushed me into a small room at the back of the house. They locked me inside.

The room was dark. There was one small window with metal bars on it.

I could eat those bars, I realized. If I could reach them.

But I was stuck on the floor. I couldn't move inside the tight net.

I lay still for a long time, waiting for something to happen. But no one returned to the room. I couldn't hear what they were doing in the other rooms.

Through the window I saw the light fading. Night was coming.

I knew there was nothing I could do but fall asleep — fall asleep and hope I'd wake up human again.

20

I woke up groggy. My stomach hurt.

Man, I thought. What did I eat yesterday? It feels as if I've got a big lump of metal in my stomach!

Then I remembered. I *did* have metal in my stomach.

Oh, yeah. I had snacked on a compact car. Mom always told me not to eat too many snacks.

I've got to remember not to do *that* again.

I sat up. I checked myself out.

Whew. I was human again.

What a relief.

The net lay open around me. Someone had cut it off while I was sleeping.

But who was I now?

My arms and legs were skinny. My feet were floppy and too big for my legs.

But they weren't *that* big. Not monster big. I was a boy again. But not my usual twelve-year-old self.

I figured I was about fourteen.

Well, I thought, it's better than being a monster. A *lot* better.

But I'm still in that house in the woods, I realized. I'm still a prisoner.

Those two guys in black had finally caught me.

What did they want? What were they going to do to me?

I stood up and tried the door. Locked.

I glanced at the window. There was no way I could break through those bars.

I was trapped.

I heard a key in the lock. They were coming!

I cowered in a corner of the room.

The door swung open. Lacie and the two guys stepped in.

"Matt?" Lacie said. She spotted me in the corner. She took a step toward me.

"What are you going to do to me?" I asked.

It was good to hear words coming out of my mouth again. Instead of just roars.

"Let me go!" I cried.

The guys in black shook their heads.

"We can't do that," the shorter guy said. "We can't let you go."

They stepped closer. They balled their hands into fists.

"No!" I shouted. "Stay away from me!"

The tall guy slammed the door shut. Then they moved in on me.

21

They walked steadily toward me. I glanced frantically around the room for a way to escape.

The guys blocked my path to the door. There was no way out.

"We're not going to hurt you, Matt," Lacie said gently. "We want to help you. Really."

The guys took another step toward me. I shrank back. They sure didn't *look* like they wanted to help me.

"Don't be afraid, Matt," Lacie said. "We need to talk to you."

She sat down in front of me. She was trying to show me I shouldn't be afraid.

But the two guys stood guard on either side of her.

"Tell me what's happening to me," I demanded.

Lacie cleared her throat. "You're trapped in a Reality Warp," she explained.

As if I'd know what she was talking about.

"Oh, of course. A Reality Warp," I cracked. "I knew *something* weird was going on."

"Cut the comedy," the shorter guy snarled. "This is no joke. You're causing us a lot of trouble."

Lacie hushed him. "Quiet, Wayne. I'll handle this."

She turned back to me and asked in her soft voice, "You don't know what a Reality Warp is, do you?"

"No," I replied. "But I know I don't like it."

"When you fell asleep in your guest room, you fell into a hole in reality," she said.

The more she told me, the less it made sense. "There's a hole in reality — in the guest room?"

She nodded. "You fell asleep in one reality, and woke up in another. You've been stuck in that hole ever since. Now, whenever you go to sleep, you change what is real and what isn't real."

"Well, make it stop!" I demanded.

"I'll stop *you*," the tall guy threatened.

"Bruce — please," Lacie snapped.

"What does all this have to do with you, anyway?" I asked.

"You're breaking the law, Matt," she said. "Every time you change, you break the laws of reality."

"I'm not doing it on purpose!" I protested. "I never even heard of the laws of reality! I'm innocent!"

Lacie tried to soothe me. "I know you're not doing it on purpose. But it doesn't matter. It's happening. When you change bodies, you change what is real and what isn't real for a lot of people. If you keep changing, you'll throw the whole world into confusion."

"You don't understand!" I cried. "I want to stop it! I'll do anything to stop it! I just want to be normal again!"

"Don't worry," Wayne murmured. "We're going to stop it."

"We're the Reality Police," Lacie told me. "Our job is to keep reality under control. We've been trying to keep up with you, Matt. It hasn't been easy, with all the changes you've made."

"But why?" I asked. "What are you going to do?"

"We had to capture you," Lacie said. "We can't allow you to break the reality laws."

I thought quickly. "It's the guest room, right? This all happened because I slept in the guest room?"

"Well —"

"I'll never sleep in the guest room again!" I promised. "I don't mind if I don't change back to my old self. This skinny fourteen-year-old body is not so bad."

Lacie shook her head. "It's too late for that, Matt. You're trapped in the hole. It doesn't matter whether you sleep in the guest room or not.

Every time you go to sleep — and wake up —
you change reality. No matter where you are."

"You mean — I can never fall asleep again?"

"That's not quite it." Lacie glanced at the two
guys. Then she trained her blue eyes on me.

"I'm sorry, Matt. I really am. You seem like a
nice guy."

An icy chill slithered down my spine. "What —
what are you talking about?"

She patted my hand. "We have no choice, Matt.
We have to put you to sleep — forever."

22

I stared at her in horror.

"You — you can't do that!" I stammered.

"Oh, yes, we can," Wayne said.

"And we will," Bruce added.

"No!" I shouted. I leaped to my feet and dove for the door. But Bruce and Wayne were ready for me. They grabbed me and held my arms behind my back.

"You're not going anywhere, kid," Wayne said.

"Let go of me!" I screamed.

I struggled and squirmed. But I wasn't a gigantic monster anymore. I was a scrawny kid — no match for Bruce and Wayne. Even Lacie probably could have beaten me up if she wanted to.

The guys tossed me against the back wall of the room.

"We'll be back later," Lacie promised. "Try not to worry about it too much, Matt. It won't hurt."

They left the room. I heard the key turn in the lock.

I was trapped again.

I searched the room for a way to escape. It was completely empty — no furniture at all, not even a chair. Just four bare walls, a locked door, and a small window with metal bars.

I opened the window and rattled the bars. I hoped they might be loose or something. But they didn't budge.

It was like being in jail. Jailed by the Reality Police.

I put my ear to the door, listening. I could hear Lacie, Bruce, and Wayne talking in the other room.

"He'll have to drink the sleeping potion," Wayne said. "Make sure he drinks the whole cup — or he might wake up."

"But what if he spits it out?" Lacie asked. "What if he doesn't swallow it?"

"I'll make him swallow it," Bruce vowed.

Yikes! I couldn't listen anymore. I frantically paced the room.

They were going to feed me a sleeping potion! To make me sleep forever!

I'd been in trouble before. My day in high school had seemed scary at the time. Being a monster was scary too. But, now — now I was really done for.

I've got to find a way out of this mess! I told myself. But how? How?

Then it dawned on me. How did I get out of trouble before?

I fell asleep. And the problem went away.

True, I always woke up with new, worse problems. But nothing could be worse than this!

Maybe, I hoped, if I fall asleep, I'll wake up somewhere else. And that's how I can escape!

I paced some more.

The only trouble was — how could I fall asleep? I was so terrified!

I knew I had to try, anyway. So I lay down on the floor. There was no bed, no pillow, no blanket. Daylight streamed in through the barred window.

Falling asleep wasn't going to be easy.

You can do it, I told myself. I remembered how my mom — my real mom — used to say I could fall asleep in a hurricane. I'm a good sleeper, it's true.

I missed my mom. It seemed like I hadn't seen her in a long, long time.

If only there were some way I could bring her back, I thought as I closed my eyes.

When I was very little, she used to sing me to sleep. I remembered the lullaby she sang. It was all about pretty ponies. . . .

I hummed the song to myself. Before I knew it, I drifted off to sleep.

23

I opened my eyes. I rubbed them. Had I fallen asleep?

Yes.

Where was I?

I looked up. Plain ceiling.

I looked around. Bare walls.

A door.

A window. With bars on it.

"No!" I cried, furious. "No!"

I was still in the same room, in the same house in the woods.

I was still a prisoner.

My plan didn't work.

Now what could I do?

"Nooooooo!"

I was so angry, so frustrated, so scared, I jumped up and down in a rage.

My plan hadn't worked. I had no more ideas. I didn't know what to do.

Now I knew for sure there was no escape for me.

I was doomed.

I heard Lacie and the two guys in the other room. They were getting the sleeping potion ready.

They'd put me to sleep forever. I'd never see my mother, or Greg, or Pam again.

How could they do this to me? It wasn't fair!

I didn't do anything wrong. Not on purpose, anyway!

Thinking about all this made me angrier and angrier. I screamed, "NOOOOOOOOOOO!"

And it sounded strange to me.

I screamed again, not so loud this time.

"Nooooo!"

I thought I was saying, "No." But that's not what I heard.

I heard a squeak.

"No!" I said again.

"*Eee!*" I heard.

It was my voice. But it wasn't a human voice.

I looked at myself. I'd forgotten to do that. I'd been so terrified to find myself still trapped — I didn't think that maybe I had changed.

But I *had* changed.

I was small. About eight inches tall.

I had tiny little paws. Gray fur. A big bushy tail.

I was a squirrel!

My eyes went to the window. I could easily squeeze through the bars now.

I didn't waste a second. I scampered up the wall and wriggled through the bars.

I was free!

Yippee! I did a little squirrel somersault to celebrate.

Then I ran through the woods as fast as I could. I found the path to town.

I scurried through town on my little squirrel feet. It seemed to take a long time. Short distances felt longer to me.

All was quiet in town. Normal. No sign that a monster had ever stomped through, chomping on cars.

I guess that reality disappeared, I thought.

This is the new reality. I'm a squirrel.

But at least I'm an *awake* squirrel. It's better than being a boy who has to sleep forever.

I sniffed the air. I had an amazing sense of smell. I thought I could smell my house from the middle of town.

I raced across the street. But I forgot what my mother always told me.

Look both ways before you cross.

A car peeled around the corner. The driver couldn't see me.

Huge black tires bore down on me. I tried to scurry out of the way.

But I didn't have time.

I shut my eyes. Is this how I'll end up? I wondered.

As roadkill?

24

SCREECH!

The driver slammed on the brakes. The car squealed to a stop.

Then everything was quiet.

I opened my eyes. One tire came so close, it touched my ear.

I zipped out from under the tire and across the street. The car sped away.

I reached the sidewalk. A dog stood guard in a yard. He barked at me.

Whoops! I dodged him and ran up a tree. The dog chased me, barking furiously.

I camped out in that tree until the dog got bored. His owner called him. He trotted away.

I sneaked out of the tree and dashed through the yard.

The rest of the way home I dodged cars, bikes, people, dogs, cats . . .

Then, at last, I found myself staring up at my

house. It was nothing special, my house. Just a white square house with peeling paint.

But it looked beautiful to me.

I had a new plan. An idea that would stop this craziness once and for all.

I hoped.

My whole problem had started when I slept in the guest room, I knew. That's where the hole in reality was — Lacie had said so.

But ever since then — ever since I slept in the guest room — I hadn't slept in my own room. Not once.

Something always stopped me. Either someone else was sleeping there, or it was being used for something else.

My own room was where I slept when my life was normal. My tiny old room. I never thought I'd miss it.

I decided I *had* to sleep in my old room again. Maybe that way, I could turn everything back to normal. The way it used to be.

I knew it sounded stupid. But it was worth a try. And, anyway, I didn't have any other ideas.

I scampered up the rain gutter to the second floor. I peeked through my old bedroom window.

There it was! My old room. With my bed in it and everything!

But the window was closed. I tried to push it with my tiny squirrel paws. No luck.

I checked the other windows in the house. They were all shut.

There had to be another way to get in. Maybe I could sneak through the door somehow.

Was anyone home? I peered through the living room window.

Mom! And Pam and Greg!

They were back!

I got so excited, I hopped up and down. I chirruped and chittered.

Then Biggie waddled into the room.

Oh, yeah. I'd forgotten about Biggie. I wasn't too glad to see him right then.

Biggie loved to chase squirrels.

He saw me right away and started barking.

Pam looked up. She smiled and pointed at me.

Yes! I thought. Come and get me, Pam. Open the window and let me in!

She gently opened the window. "Here, little squirrel," she cooed. "You're so cute!"

I hesitated. I wanted to go inside. But Biggie was barking like crazy.

"Put Biggie in the basement!" Pam told Greg. "He's scaring the squirrel."

She was being nicer to me as a squirrel than she ever was to her little brother. But I let that slide for now.

Greg led Biggie to the basement and shut the door.

"Come on, squirrel," Pam chirped. "It's safe now."

I hopped into the house.

"Look!" Pam cried. "He wants to come in! It's almost like he's tame!"

"Don't let him in here!" Mom warned. "Those animals have rabies! Or bugs, at the very least."

I tried not to listen. It's hard to hear your own mother insult you that way.

I focused on getting upstairs. If I could only get up to my room and fall asleep, just for a few minutes. . . .

"He's getting away!" Greg shouted. "Catch him!"

Pam pounced at me. I skittered away.

"If that squirrel gets lost in this house, Pamela," Mom warned, "you're going to be in big, big trouble."

"I'll catch him," Pam promised.

Not if I can help it, I silently vowed.

Pam cut me off at the stairs. I darted into the kitchen.

Pam followed. She closed the kitchen door behind her.

I was trapped.

"Here, little squirrel," she called. "Here, boy."

I twitched my tail. I searched the room for a way out.

Pam inched her way toward me. She was trying not to scare me away.

I scurried under the table. She dove for me. Missed.

But when I scampered away, she cornered me.

And snatched me up.

I never knew she was so speedy.

She grabbed me by the neck and held my feet together. "I got him!" she shouted.

Greg threw open the kitchen door. Mom stood behind him.

"Take him outside — quick!" Mom ordered.

"Can't I keep him, Mom?" Pam begged. "He'd be such a cute pet!"

I shuddered. Me, as Pam's pet! What a nightmare!

But it might be my best chance to get back to my room.

"No!" Mom insisted. "You absolutely cannot keep him. Put him outside — now."

Pam's mouth drooped. "Okay, Mom," she said sadly. "Whatever you say."

She carried me out of the kitchen. "Mom is so mean," she said loudly so Mom could hear her. "All I wanted to do was pet you and cuddle you for a while. What's wrong with that?"

A lot, I thought. Pam was the last person I wanted petting and cuddling me. Except for Greg.

She opened the front door. "Bye, you cute little squirrel," she said.

Then she slammed the door shut.

But she didn't let me go. She held me tightly in her arms.

Then she slipped upstairs to her room.

"Don't worry, squirrel," she whispered. "I won't keep you very long. Just a little while."

She pulled something out from under her bed. Her old hamster cage.

She opened the door of the cage. She shoved me inside.

"No!" I protested. But all I could do was squeak.

She locked the latch.

I was a prisoner again!

25

Now what am I going to do? I thought frantically. I'm stuck in this stupid cage. I can't talk.

How will I ever get to my old room?

Another bad thought came to me.

If I fell asleep in this tiny hamster cage — what would happen when I woke up?

Pam's big face loomed over the cage. "Are you hungry, squirrely-kins? I'll go get you some nuts or something."

She left the room for a minute. I paced the cage, thinking hard. The next thing I knew, I was running on the hamster wheel.

Stop it! I told myself. I made myself get off the wheel. I didn't want to get used to being a rodent.

"Here you go, squirrel." Pam had returned to the room with a handful of nuts. She opened the door to the cage and sprinkled the nuts inside.

"Yum yum!" she squealed.

Oh, brother.

I ate the nuts. I was very hungry after all my

adventures. But I would have enjoyed them more if Pam hadn't watched me the whole time.

The phone rang. A moment later I heard Greg call, "Pam! Telephone!"

"Excellent!" Pam cried. She jumped up and ran out of the room.

Like a moron, I sat there gobbling nuts. It took me five minutes to notice that Pam had left the cage door unlatched.

"Yes!" I squeaked. For once I was glad that Pam was no genius.

I pushed the door open with my paws. I crept toward the bedroom door, listening for footsteps.

The coast was clear. Now was my chance!

I dashed out the door. Down the hall. To my room.

The door was shut. I threw my tiny squirrel body against it, trying to open it.

No way. It was closed tight.

Rats!

I heard footsteps down the hall. Pam was coming back!

I knew I had to get out of there before Pam put me back in that cage.

Or before my mother swatted me with a broom.

I scurried down the steps and into the living room.

Was the window still open? Yes.

I ran behind the couch, along the wall, under a chair . . .

Then I leaped up to the windowsill and out into the yard.

I climbed a tree and curled up on a branch to rest.

I couldn't get into my old room as a squirrel. There was only one thing I could do.

I had to go to sleep again. And this time, I'd better wake up as a human.

Because I had to get to my old room. If I didn't, I'd be in trouble.

Big trouble.

The Reality Police were on my trail. It was only a matter of time before they'd find me.

If they did, nothing could save me.

26

CRASH! THUD!

OOF!

I landed hard on the ground. What a way to wake up.

Who was I this time?

What a relief. I was a twelve-year-old boy again. But I still wasn't my old self.

I was a very, very chubby boy. A real blimp. No wonder the tree branch didn't hold me.

But that didn't matter. I was a human again. I could talk.

And maybe now I could get to my old room at last.

I marched straight up to the front door and tried the knob.

Locked.

So I knocked.

I had no idea who would answer. I hoped it wasn't a monster family.

The door opened.

"Mom!" I cried. I was so glad to see her. "Mom — it's me! Matt!"

Mom stared at me. "Who are you?" she asked.

"Matt! Matt, Mom! Your son!"

She squinted at me. "Matt? I don't know anyone named Matt," she said.

"Sure you do, Mom! Don't you remember me? Remember that lullaby you used to sing to me when I was a baby?"

She narrowed her eyes suspiciously.

Greg and Pam appeared behind her. "Who is it, Mom?" Pam asked.

"Greg!" I shouted. "Pam! It's me, Matt! I'm back!"

"Who is this kid?" Greg asked.

"I don't know him," Pam said.

Oh, no, I thought. Please don't let this be happening. I'm so close. . . .

"I need to sleep in my old room," I begged. "Please, Mom. Let me go upstairs and sleep in my room. It's a matter of life and death!"

"I don't know you," Mom said. "And I don't know any Matt. You have the wrong house."

"This kid is some kind of wacko," Greg said.

"Mom! Wait!" I cried.

Mom slammed the door in my face.

I turned around and started down the walk. What do I do now? I wondered.

Then I stopped. I glanced down the block.

Three people were running toward me. The last three people I wanted to see.

Lacie, Bruce, and Wayne.

The Reality Police! They'd found me!

27

"There he is!" Lacie pointed at me. The three of them started to run.

"Get him!"

I turned and ran. It wasn't easy. I couldn't run very fast.

Why did I have to wake up chubby this time?

I did have one advantage. I knew the neighborhood inside out — and they didn't. I ran across the yard to the next-door neighbor's house.

I glanced back. The Reality Police were gaining on me. They were half a block away.

I disappeared behind the neighbor's house. Then I sneaked back around to my house.

At the back of the garage is a line of thick shrubs. I threw myself behind the shrubs and held my breath.

A few minutes later, three pairs of feet hurried past me.

"Where'd he go?" I heard Lacie ask.

"He must've gone the other way," Wayne said. "Come on!"

They ran off.

Whew. I could breathe again. I let out a whoosh of air.

Safe for now. But I knew the Reality Police would find me again.

I had to get back to my room. But there was no way Mom would let me in. She thought I was a total nutcase.

There was only one thing to do. I had to break into the house.

I'd wait until nighttime. Till everyone was asleep.

Then I'd find an open window somewhere — or break one if I had to.

I'd sneak into my room and sleep there. I hoped I wouldn't find someone else sleeping there.

In the meantime, I had to wait for night. I stayed hidden behind the shrubs. I lay as still as I could.

And I struggled to stay awake. I didn't want to fall asleep again.

If I fell asleep, who knew what I'd be? I might never get to my room.

The hours ticked slowly by. At last night came. The neighborhood got quiet.

I pulled myself out of the shrubs. My legs and arms ached from hiding.

I looked at the house. Everyone had gone to bed, except for Mom. Her bedroom light was still on.

I waited until it went off. I waited another half hour to give her time to fall sound asleep.

Then I crept around to the front of the house. My room was on the second floor.

I knew Mom had locked all the doors. I knew she'd locked all the first-floor windows. She did that every night.

I had to climb to the second floor and sneak in through my window. It was the only way.

I had to climb up the tree that grew by my window. Then reach out and grab the rain gutter.

Then set myself down on the narrow ledge outside my window. I'd have to cling to the gutter for balance.

If I could make it to the ledge, I might be able to open the window and crawl in.

That was the plan, anyway. The more I thought about it, the more stupid it sounded.

Better not think about it, then, I decided. Just do it.

I stood up on my toes, stretching toward the lowest branch of the tree. It was just out of reach. I'd have to jump.

I bent my knees and sprang up. My fingertips grazed the branch, but I couldn't get a grip on it.

If only I weren't so chubby! I could barely get off the ground.

I won't give up, I vowed. If this doesn't work, I'm doomed.

So I took a deep breath. I gathered all my strength.

I crouched down. I sprang up as high as I could.

Yes! I grabbed the branch!

I hung there for a second, wriggling. I kicked my legs. They were so heavy!

I twisted around and walked my legs up the tree trunk. With a grunt of effort, I hoisted myself onto the branch.

Whew.

The rest of the tree was pretty easy. I climbed up until I reached the branch just outside my window.

I grabbed a branch over my head as I stood up. I could just reach the rain gutter. I sure hoped it would hold.

I grasped the gutter. I tried to put my foot on the window ledge.

I missed.

I was hanging by my fingertips from the gutter!

I looked down. The ground seemed far away.

I squeezed my lips shut to keep myself from screaming.

I panted, hanging there. I had to get my foot on that ledge — or I'd fall.

I wriggled to the left, trying to get closer to the ledge.

CRACK!

What was that?

CRACK!

The gutter! It wasn't going to hold!

28

CRACK!

I felt myself sink. The gutter was about to give way.

I mustered all my strength. Clinging to the gutter, I stretched one leg out as far as it would go. My toes touched the window ledge.

I set one foot down. Then the other.

I made it!

I crouched on the ledge. I clung to the gutter with one hand, for balance.

I didn't move. I tried to catch my breath. The night was cool. But I felt drops of sweat trickle down my face. I wiped them away with my free hand.

I peered through the window. My room was dark. Was anybody in there?

I couldn't tell.

The window was shut.

Please don't let it be locked, I prayed.

If I couldn't get in, I'd be stuck up on the ledge. I'd have no way to get down.

Unless I fell down, of course.

I carefully tried the window. It slid up. It wasn't locked!

I pushed it open. Then I crawled into the room. I tumbled onto the floor.

I froze. Did anyone hear me?

No sounds. Everyone was still asleep.

I pulled myself to my feet. There was my bed! My old bed! And it was empty!

I was so happy, I wanted to jump up and shout. But I didn't.

I'll save the celebration for tomorrow, I decided. If my plan works.

I took off my shoes and crawled into bed. I sighed. Clean sheets.

It felt good to be back. Everything was almost normal.

I was sleeping in my own bed. Mom and Pam and Greg were all asleep in their rooms.

Okay, I didn't look like myself. I didn't have my old body back yet.

And my family didn't recognize me. If they saw me now, they'd think I was a burglar. Or a maniac.

I pushed those things out of my mind. I wanted to think about the morning.

What will happen tomorrow? I wondered sleepily.

Who will I be when I wake up? Will my life be normal again?

Or will I find Lacie and those two guys standing over me, ready to pounce?

There was only one way to find out. I closed my eyes and drifted off to sleep.

29

I felt something warm on my face. Sunlight.

I opened my eyes. Where was I?

I glanced around. I was in a small, cramped, messy room full of junk.

My old room!

My heart skipped a beat. Did my plan work? Was I back to normal?

I couldn't wait to find out. I threw off the covers and jumped out of bed. I hurried to the mirror on the back of my bedroom door.

I saw a skinny, blond, twelve-year-old boy. Yes! I was back!

I was me again!

"Woo-hoo!" I cried.

Biggie nosed the door open and waddled into the room. He growled at me. He barked.

"Biggie!" I cried happily. I bent down and hugged him. He snapped at me.

Good old Biggie.

"Matt!" I heard Mom's voice call from the kitchen. My *real* mom's voice.

"Matt! Leave Biggie alone! Stop teasing him!"

"I'm not teasing him!" I yelled back. She always blames me for everything.

But I didn't care! I was so glad to be back!

I scrambled downstairs for breakfast.

There they sat. Mom. Pam. Greg. Just the way I left them.

"The geek enters the kitchen for his morning feeding," Greg spoke into his tape recorder. "What does a geek eat? Let's watch and find out."

"Greg!" I sang. I threw my arms around his neck and hugged him.

"Hey!" He swatted me away. "Get off me, geek!"

"And Pam!" I gave her a big hug too.

"What's your problem, pea-brain?" she snapped. "I know — you got kidnapped by aliens last night! Am I right? And they brainwashed you!"

I ignored her jokes. I patted the top of her Brillo pad hair.

"Cut it out!" she whined.

I gave my mom the biggest hug of all.

"Thanks, honey." She patted me on the back. At least *she* was on my side, once in a while.

"Get some cereal, Matt," she said. "I'm running late."

I sighed happily and fixed myself some cereal. Everything was back to normal. No one even noticed I'd been gone.

I'm never going into that stupid guest room again, I vowed. Never. I'm going to stay in my little room from now on — no matter how cramped it gets.

THWACK! Something stung me on the back of the neck.

I whirled around. Greg grinned at me. He held a straw in one hand.

He spoke into the tape recorder. "What happens if you shoot a paper wad at the geek? How does he respond?"

"I bet he cries like a baby," Pam said.

I shrugged and went back to my cereal. "You can't bother me," I said. "I'm too happy."

Pam and Greg exchanged glances. Pam twirled one finger at the side of her head. It was the international signal for "He's nuts."

"Something has happened to the geek," Greg announced.

"Yeah," Pam agreed. "The geek has changed."

School was so much fun that day. It was great to be in seventh grade again. So much easier than high school.

We played soccer in gym. I even scored a goal.

But on my way to my last class, I saw something that made my heart stop.

A girl walking down the hall. About my age. Long, thick blond hair in a ponytail.

Oh, no.

Lacie!

I froze. What should I do?

Were the Reality Police still after me? I had fixed everything! They didn't need to put me to sleep anymore!

I've got to get out of here, I decided. I got ready to run.

Then the girl turned around. She grinned at me.

It wasn't Lacie. Just some girl with long blond hair.

I took a deep breath. I need to relax, I thought. It's over now. It was all a bad dream. Sort of.

The girl walked away. I went to my last class. No sign of Lacie, Bruce, or Wayne anywhere.

I whistled all the way home, thinking about how easy my homework was going to be.

I walked into the house. "Hi, Matt!" Mom called.

"Mom?" I was surprised to see her. She was usually at work when I got home. "What are you doing home so early?"

She smiled at me. "I took the day off," she explained. "I had a few things to do around the house."

"Oh." I shrugged and turned on the TV.

Mom switched it off. "Matt — aren't you curious?"

"Curious? About what?"

"About what I've been doing all day?"

I glanced around the living room. Everything looked the same.

"I don't know," I said. "What have you been doing?"

She smiled again. She looked excited about something.

"Have you forgotten?" she said. "It's your birthday this week!"

Actually, I *had* forgotten. So much weird stuff had been going on.

When you're running for your life, you don't think much about your birthday.

"I have a special surprise for you," Mom said. "Come upstairs and I'll show you."

I followed her upstairs. I started getting excited. What could the surprise be?

It wasn't like Mom to make such a big deal about my birthday. The surprise must be something really great, I decided.

She stopped in front of my bedroom door.

"Is the surprise in my room?" I asked.

"Look." She pushed open the door.

I peered inside. My room was filled with cartons. Big boxes from floor to ceiling.

Wow!

"Are all those presents for me?" I asked.

Mom laughed. "Presents? All those boxes? Of course not!" She cracked up.

I knew it had to be too good to be true.

"Well — what's the surprise, then?" I asked.

"Matt," she began, "I've been thinking about what you said the other day. And I decided you were right. Your room is too small for you. So I've turned it into a storage closet."

"You — you what?"

"That's right." She walked across the hall.

She threw open the guest room door. "Ta-da!"

No. Oh, no.

It can't be. Not that.

"Happy Birthday, Matt!" Mom shouted. "Welcome to your new room!"

"Uh . . . uh . . . uh . . ." I couldn't say a word.

My bed, my dresser, all my posters and books — they were all set up in the guest room.

"Matt? What's the matter?" Mom cried. "This is what you said you wanted!"

My mouth fell open. I started to scream.

About R.L. Stine

R.L. Stine is the most popular author in America. He is the creator of the *Goosebumps, Give Yourself Goosebumps, Fear Street,* and *Ghosts of Fear Street* series, among other popular books. He has written more than one hundred scary novels for kids. Bob lives in New York City with his wife, Jane, teenage son, Matt, and dog, Nadine.

Add *more*

Goosebumps®

to your collection . . .
A chilling preview of
what's next from
R.L. STINE

THE BLOB THAT ATE EVERYONE

20

... "It's true!" I insisted. "Adam, I just proved it to you."

He laughed and rolled his eyes.

I wanted to punch his laughing face. I really did.

Here was the most amazing thing that ever happened to anyone in the history of the world — and he thought it was a big joke!

I grabbed his arm. "Here," I said breathlessly. "I'll prove it again. Watch."

I dragged him to the typewriter.

I didn't bother to sit down. I leaned over the desk and started to type something.

But before I had typed two words, Alex tugged me away.

"What are you *doing*?" I cried. I struggled to break away. But she pulled me out to the hall.

"He's not going to believe us, Zackie," she whispered. "You can prove it to him a dozen times, and he won't believe it."

"Of course he will!" I insisted. "He'll —"

"No way," Alex interrupted. "Go ahead. Type ADAM HAS TWO HEADS. If you do it, *both* of his heads won't believe you!"

I had to think about that one.

"One more try," I said. "Let me type one more sentence. When Adam sees it come true, maybe he'll change his mind. Maybe he'll see it isn't a joke."

Alex shrugged. "Go ahead. But he has his mind made up, Zackie. He thinks you're trying to pay him back for the monster costume."

"One more try," I insisted.

I glanced into the room. "No — ! Adam — stop!" I shrieked.

He had his back turned to us. But I could see that he was leaning over the typewriter.

He was typing something onto the page!

"Adam — stop!" Alex and I both wailed.

We dove into the room.

He spun around, a wide grin on his face. "I've got to go!" he exclaimed.

He swept past us and out into the hall. "So long, suckers!" he called. He disappeared down the hall.

I hurtled to the desk. My heart pounding, I stared down at the typewriter.

What did Adam type?

21

I heard the front door slam. Adam had run out of the house.

I didn't care about Adam now. I only cared about one thing.

What did he type on the old typewriter?

I grabbed the sheet of paper — and pulled it from the roller. Then I held it close to a candle flame to read it.

"Careful! You'll set it on fire!" Alex warned.

I moved it back from the flame. Orange light flickered over the page. My hand was trembling so hard, I struggled to read it.

"Well? What did he type?" Alex asked impatiently.

"He — he — he —" I sputtered.

She grabbed the paper from my hand and read Adam's sentence out loud:

"THE BLOB MONSTER HID IN ZACKIE'S BASEMENT, WAITING FOR FRESH MEAT."

"What a jerk!" I cried. "I don't believe him! Why did he type that on my story?"

Alex stared unhappily at the page. "He thought it was funny."

"Ha-ha," I said weakly. I grabbed the page back from her. "He ruined my story. Now I have to start it all over again."

"Forget your story. What about the Blob Monster?" Alex cried.

"Huh?" A chill tightened the back of my neck. The sheet of paper slipped from my hand.

"Everything typed on the old typewriter comes true," Alex murmured.

I was so upset about Adam ruining my story that I forgot!

"You mean — ?" I started. My mouth suddenly felt very dry.

"There is a Blob Monster waiting in the basement," Alex said, in a low whisper. "Waiting for fresh meat."

"Fresh meat," I repeated. I gulped.

Alex and I froze for a moment, staring at each other in the darting candlelight.

"But there is no such thing as a Blob Monster," I said finally. "I made it up. So how can a Blob Monster be hiding in my basement?"

Alex's eyes flashed behind her glasses. "You're right!" she cried. "They don't exist! So . . . no problem!" She smiled.

But her smile faded when we heard a noise.

A heavy *THUD THUD*.

I gasped. "What was *that*?"

We both turned to the door.

And heard the sound again. *THUD THUD*.

Heavy and slow. Like footsteps.

"Is it . . . is it coming from downstairs?" I choked out.

Alex nodded. "The basement," she whispered.

I picked up a candlestick. The light bounced over the wall and floor. I couldn't stop my hand from shaking.

Holding it in front of me, I made my way into the hall.

Alex huddled close, keeping with me step for step.

Thud THUD.

We both stopped. The sounds were closer. Louder.

Taking a deep breath, I stepped up to the basement door.

Alex hung back, her hands pressed to her face. Behind her glasses, her eyes were wide with fear.

THUD THUD.

"It's coming up the stairs!" I cried. "Run!"

Too late.

I heard another *THUD* — and the door crashed open.

This Blob Is a Total Slob!

Goosebumps®

Zackie likes writing horror stories. So when he gets a typewriter—for free—he's psyched. But this typewriter is strange. When Zackie types something—it happens in real life! Like the Blob Monster in the basement! Can Zackie handle this hungry monster before it makes a meal out of the entire town?

The Blob That Ate Everyone

Goosebumps #55

R.L. Stine

Ooozing into a bookstore near you!

GBT996

© 1997 Parachute Press, Inc. GOOSEBUMPS is a registered trademark of Parachute Press, Inc. All rights reserved.

R.L. STINE
GIVE YOURSELF
Goosebumps®

These Comics Are No Joke!

You discovered Milo's Comic Dungeon in a bad part of town. It's really dark and dirty—but who cares, there are hundreds of awesome comics! And nobody's around. Right? WRONG!

If you decide to go downstairs you tumble into the basement. Now you're a "test subject" of Milo the Mutant. If you go upstairs, you step into comic book land and battle freaky monsters. Do you have what it takes to become a comic book hero?

Choose from more than 20 eerie endings!

Give Yourself Goosebumps #17
Little Comic
Shop of Horrors

Coming soon to a bookstore near you!

© 1997 Parachute Press, Inc. GOOSEBUMPS is a registered trademark of Parachute Press, Inc. All rights reserved. GYGB996

CHILLING STORIES BASED ON THE FOX KIDS TV SHOW

R.L. STINE

Goosebumps®

PRESENTS

TV BOOK #12

Skip loves reading *The Masked Mutant.* It's his favorite comic book. But now someone's drawn him into the comic! Can an ordinary boy defeat the evil Masked Mutant? Or will the evil Masked Mutant make mincemeat out of Skipper?

Goosebumps Presents
TV Episode #12

Attack of the Mutant

by R.L. Stine

With 8 pages of full-color photos from the show!

Look for it in a bookstore near you!

© 1997 Parachute Press, Inc. GOOSEBUMPS is a registered trademark of Parachute Press, Inc. All rights reserved.   GBTV996

THE LATEST IN SCARE WEAR!

Goosebumps®

Book and Cap Pack

SCARY STORIES!
COOL CAP!

Matt gets a cool new lunch box—
full of monsters! A girl finds a pair
of cat-eye glasses—that send her
back in time! You get *More & More
Tales to Give You Goosebumps*, a
collection of ten new super-scary
stories, *plus* an awesome
Goosebumps cap!

Look for it at your
local bookstore!

◢SCHOLASTIC   GBSS996

It's here!

Goosebumps ™

the CD-ROM GAME,
where you dodge Mutants, Weirdos
and Creatures that Drool.
(Just like the hallways at school.)

"Escape from Horrorland™"
Available at your local software store.

DREAMWORKS INTERACTIVE

Based on
your favorite
"Goosebumps"
Books.

TM & © 1996 Parachute Press, Inc.

GOT Goosebumps YET?

by R.L. Stine

───── GOOSEBUMPS ─────

❑ BAB45365-3	#1	Welcome to Dead House	$3.99
❑ BAB45366-1	#2	Stay Out of the Basement	$3.99
❑ BAB45367-X	#3	Monster Blood	$3.99
❑ BAB45368-8	#4	Say Cheese and Die!	$3.99
❑ BAB45369-6	#5	The Curse of the Mummy's Tomb	$3.99
❑ BAB49445-7	#10	The Ghost Next Door	$3.99
❑ BAB49450-3	#15	You Can't Scare Me!	$3.99
❑ BAB47742-0	#20	The Scarecrow Walks at Midnight	$3.99
❑ BAB48355-2	#25	Attack of the Mutant	$3.99
❑ BAB48348-X	#30	It Came from Beneath the Sink	$3.99
❑ BAB48349-8	#31	The Night of the Living Dummy II	$3.99
❑ BAB48344-7	#32	The Barking Ghost	$3.99
❑ BAB48345-5	#33	The Horror at Camp Jellyjam	$3.99
❑ BAB48346-3	#34	Revenge of the Lawn Gnomes	$3.99
❑ BAB48340-4	#35	A Shocker on Shock Street	$3.99
❑ BAB56873-6	#36	The Haunted Mask II	$3.99
❑ BAB56874-4	#37	The Headless Ghost	$3.99
❑ BAB56875-2	#38	The Abominable Snowman of Pasadena	$3.99
❑ BAB56876-0	#39	How I Got My Shrunken Head	$3.99
❑ BAB56877-9	#40	Night of the Living Dummy III	$3.99
❑ BAB56878-7	#41	Bad Hare Day	$3.99
❑ BAB56879-5	#42	Egg Monsters from Mars	$3.99
❑ BAB56880-9	#43	The Beast from the East	$3.99
❑ BAB56881-7	#44	Say Cheese and Die–Again!	$3.99
❑ BAB56882-5	#45	Ghost Camp	$3.99
❑ BAB56883-3	#46	How to Kill a Monster	$3.99
❑ BAB56884-1	#47	Legend of the Lost Legend	$3.99
❑ BAB56885-X	#48	Attack of the Jack-O'-Lanterns	$3.99
❑ BAB56886-8	#49	Vampire Breath	$3.99
❑ BAB56887-6	#50	Calling All Creeps	$3.99
❑ BAB56888-4	#51	Beware, the Snowman	$3.99
❑ BAB56889-2	#52	How I Learned to Fly	$3.99

───── GOOSEBUMPS PRESENTS ─────

❑ BAB74586-7	TV Episode #1: The Girl Who Cried Monster	$3.99
❑ BAB74587-5	TV Episode #2: The Cuckoo Clock of Doom	$3.99
❑ BAB74588-3	TV Episode #3: Welcome to Camp Nightmare	$3.99
❑ BAB74589-1	TV Episode #4: Return of the Mummy	$3.99
❑ BAB74590-5	TV Episode #5: Night of the Living Dummy II	$3.99
❑ BAB82519-4	TV Episode #6: My Hairiest Adventure	$3.99

© 1996 Parachute Press, Inc. GOOSEBUMPS is a registered trademark of Parachute Press, Inc. All rights reserved.

❑ BAB93954-8	TV Episode #7: The Headless Ghost	$3.99
❑ BAB93955-6	TV Episode #8: Be Careful What You Wish For	$3.99
❑ BAB93959-9	TV Episode #9: Go Eat Worms!	$3.99
❑ BAB62836-4	Tales to Give You Goosebumps Book & Light Set Special Edition #1	$11.95
❑ BAB26603-9	More Tales to Give You Goosebumps Book & Light Set Special Edition #2	$11.95
❑ BAB74150-4	Even More Tales to Give You Goosebumps Book and Boxer Shorts Pack Special Edition #3	$14.99

GIVE YOURSELF GOOSEBUMPS

❑ BAB55323-2	#1: Escape from the Carnival of Horrors	$3.99
❑ BAB56645-8	#2: Tick Tock, You're Dead	$3.99
❑ BAB56646-6	#3: Trapped in Bat Wing Hall	$3.99
❑ BAB67318-1	#4: The Deadly Experiments of Dr. Eeek	$3.99
❑ BAB67319-X	#5: Night in Werewolf Woods	$3.99
❑ BAB67320-3	#6: Beware of the Purple Peanut Butter	$3.99
❑ BAB67321-1	#7: Under the Magician's Spell	$3.99
❑ BAB84765-1	#8: The Curse of the Creeping Coffin	$3.99
❑ BAB84766-X	#9: The Knight in Screaming Armor	$3.99
❑ BAB84767-8	#10: Diary of a Mad Mummy	$3.99
❑ BAB84768-6	#11: Deep in the Jungle of Doom	$3.99
❑ BAB84772-4	#12: Welcome to the Wicked Wax Museum	$3.99
❑ BAB84773-2	#13: Scream of the Evil Genie	$3.99
❑ BAB84774-0	#14: The Creepy Creations of Professor Shock	$3.99

❑ BAB53770-9	The Goosebumps Monster Blood Pack	$11.95
❑ BAB50995-0	The Goosebumps Monster Edition #1	$12.95
❑ BAB93371-X	The Goosebumps Monster Edition #2	$12.95
❑ BAB60265-9	Goosebumps Official Collector's Caps Collecting Kit	$5.99
❑ BAB73906-9	Goosebumps Postcard Book	$7.95
❑ BAB73902-6	The 1997 Goosebumps 365 Scare-a-Day Calendar	$8.95
❑ BAB73907-7	The Goosebumps 1997 Wall Calendar	$10.99

Scare me, thrill me, mail me GOOSEBUMPS now!

Available wherever you buy books, or use this order form. Scholastic Inc., P.O. Box 7502, 2931 East McCarty Street, Jefferson City, MO 65102

Please send me the books I have checked above. I am enclosing $_____ (please add $2.00 to cover shipping and handling). Send check or money order — no cash or C.O.D.s please.

Name _____ Age _____

Address _____

City _____ State/Zip_____

Please allow four to six weeks for delivery. Offer good in the U.S. only. Sorry, mail orders are not available to residents of Canada. Prices subject to change.

YOU ASKED FOR IT!

IT CAME FROM OHIO!
My Life As A Writer

R.L. STINE
AS TOLD TO JOE ARTHUR

66 When I was four, it was my job to let our dog, Whitey, out of the garage every morning. As soon as I stepped outside, I could hear him scratching at the door. Barking and crying he would leap on me—and knock me down to the driveway. Every morning!

'Down, Whitey! Down!' I begged. THUD!

Whitey was a good dog. But I think he helped give me my scary view of life....**99**

What was your favorite author, R.L. Stine, like as a kid?
How did he start writing books?
Where does he get his scary ideas from?

Find out all about R.L. Stine in this funny biography—written in his own voice! Includes lots of never-before-seen photos and drawings from R.L. Stine's personal collection.

FIND IT AT A BOOKSTORE NEAR YOU!

RL696

A Frightfully Good Offer

Goosebumps®

GET $2.00 BACK!

Get a $2.00 rebate when you buy <u>two</u> Goosebumps books*! (Offer good on books #1– #40 <u>only</u>)

To receive your $2.00 rebate, return this coupon and your cash register receipt as proof of purchase to: Goosebumps Rebate Offer, Scholastic Inc., P.O. Box 7501, Jefferson City, MO. 65102-9997.

Name_____

Address_____

City_____State_____Zip_____

*Also valid with the purchase of <u>one</u> boxed set.
Offer expires 12/31/97. This $2.00 rebate is good with purchase only and is not redeemable for cash value. Offer valid in U.S. only.

© 1997 Parachute Press, Inc. GOOSEBUMPS is a registered trademark of Parachute Press, Inc. All rights reserved.   GBREB2